The Mystique Woven in Our Land

By

Deborah DR Kralich

The Mystique Woven in Our Land

Copyright 2016
By
Deborah DR Kralich

Published by Ruskras Corner
The United States of America

Dedicated to my mother, Mae Frances- and the branch of her ancestors
who settled in Kentucky in the late 1700s, migrating to Texas a century later...
Thank you!

ISBN 9781942542117
TX0008502160

All cover designs, artwork and photography by Deborah D Russo, copyright 2016

Cast of Characters
Their youth reflects both the new nation and the deadly times...

Abigail Fichton, 32, her role in a famous victory colors the rest of her life.

Jane Penberthy, 20, beauty of the colony, she chose wealth over love but has come to cherish her older husband.

Genevieve Brown, 33, the general's niece, she is a war widow, a writer who pens pamphlets with double meanings and letters that open doors.

Lantern Leshoward, 17, the general's daughter, she says she resists marriage because she doesn't want to be subservient to a husband but it could be she is afraid no one will want her.

Hortense Melton, 18, daughter of horse breeders, running away to the east with a lover seems to sum up her life.

Prudence Horaceton, 28, wife of the schoolmaster, stepmother to his children, she dislikes the daily routine of her life.

Thistle Mannstein, 33, widowed during the war she made a bold declaration in order to be allowed to wed her second husband, an immensely rich man.

Margaret Craig, 24, devoted to her politician husband, she schemes to keep him in power.

Naomi Short, 19, servant to a wealthy mistress, they are sisters under the skin, fellow players in life's games.

Emilia, 16, dark of skin, young of age, she knows better what she wants from life than most.

Ruthanne Webber, 28, embarking on a courtship with a man she has never met, she carries secrets from the east to the lands of Kentucky.

Hayward Manchester, 39, a Revolutionary War hero/blacksmith with a mysterious Asian background, he makes swords sought after throughout the state.

Reginald Penberthy, 45, wealthy and older, he seeks power in the new government unashamedly.

Ronald Leshoward, 47, thrust into a warrior's role that ill becomes him, presiding over death, he would rather be a benevolent governor of life.

Fabric, 19, a new life and name awaits him if he has faith to take the chance.

Shears Plate, 23, thorough and loyal, General Leshoward is like a father to him but does not want to be his father-in-law.

Henri Mannstein, 42, Catholic in a protestant land, he devotes most of his passion to his beautiful mysterious wife.

Reverend Lawrence Falldrem, 38, does not approve of the general's plan for tolerance in the town, but will abide it if he can be senior among the clergy.

Marchmont Craig, 29, a congressman delighted at his wife's pregnancy.

Father McKinsy, 39, the only priest in the colony- he has to tread lightly.

Neilman Horaceton, 23, schoolmaster to the colony, he is weary of the world.

Private Crier, 18, his is a small vital role in all the intrigue.

Prologue -1777

The enemy was upon them. Only the dark night staved off certain defeat and death.

The razor sharp sting of the snow demolished its beauty.

The winter cold was merciless to soldiers in battle.

General Ronald Leshoward wore his full uniform, dress sword, and hat, although the weather had confined him to the small interior within the tent where he slept on a small cot and ate at a large table.

A battlefield map was spread next to his food.

He was alone, pacing the small space, his sheathed sword noisily readjusting itself each time he made a complete turn and started the short walk back in the opposite direction.

He clasped his hands behind his back as he moved.

There was no hope.

The British would attack at dawn.

His small forces were heavily outnumbered.

The land he held was crucial.

The battle might not decide the war, but a loss would certainly prolong it and could tip the scales of victory to the British.

Threading through his mind were constantly changing scenarios in which the plan he had carefully formed with his subordinates the previous day actually had some hope of working.

Occasionally interwoven within the threads he would see the face of his wife as he beheld her on their wedding day, fresh and healthy, full of life.

Then this momentary glimpse of his past happiness would warm him before the cold grip of reality would override the vision and he would behold his wife's face as he had last seen her, confined to a sure bed of death.

The growth at her breast slowly sapping the life from her.

The last correspondence indicated she still lived but there was little hope she would be there when the war was over and he went home.

If he went home.

He took off his hat and ran his fingers through his thinning hair.

His hairline receding to a widow's peak had aggravated him before the war. Now it was a double-edged sword, making him look older and more authoritative to his men.

He tossed the hat on the bed.

He reached the end of the room and turned around and paced again, the prayer in his heart not spoken on his lips was that should anyone perish in defeat the next day it should be him.

The tent flap burst open and one of his lieutenants rushed him.

"There's a messenger here to see you, General. Urgent."

Apparently a boy, tall and thin, wrapped in heavy coats, a hood across his face to ward off the chill, slipped inside.

This boy looks big enough to be serving, Leshoward thought, with some irritation. *He's too old to be a messenger. Too tall.*

"Personal for the general," the messenger mumbled and jerked a hand towards the lieutenant.

"Thank you, Lieutenant, that will be all," General Leshoward said automatically. He was used to messages meant for his ears only.

The lieutenant dashed out into the pelting snow.

"Well, boy. What is the message?"

Leshoward bent over the table, looking at the map, anticipating that only a message that indicated some change in the enemy's position would be important enough to send out a young vulnerable boy on such a night.

"General Leshoward? I am confirming that is who you are."

The general whirled abruptly. His sword struck the edge of the table, shaking the whole piece of furniture.

The voice that had just addressed him was very feminine, not even to be mistaken for a young boy's voice before the change.

The messenger removed her outer coat uncovering the rest of the full-length robe. She pushed the hood back and long brown hair fell against her cheeks.

General Leshoward looked down.

The robe had been covering a dress.

"You are General Leshoward?" the woman repeated insistently.

"Yes, Mistress, Mrs." He corrected the salutation when he noticed the wedding band on her ring finger.

"Good. My husband is a private in your army."

"Madam! The battle starts tomorrow. In no way can I make any exceptions for anyone," he began.

"That is not why I'm here. I just wanted to identify myself to you as the wife of one of your soldiers so that you know my heart is completely with the Continental Army and our patriotic cause."

"Then what on earth are you doing here?"

"You must change your battle plan. Your information about the enemy is flawed. You have a good chance to win this battle if you listen to me and do what I say," said this strange woman.

"Listen to you?"

As Leshoward watched in astonishment, the woman strode over to the table of maps.

"You think that the enemy is here." She pointed. "But actually the British are in offensive position on this site."

"Madam- "

"Hear me out, General. This may be life-and-death, win-or-lose in this war. If it wasn't so crucial, I would not have risked my life and reputation to come to you tonight."

Leshoward suddenly realized he was alone with the woman with no chaperon and she was the wife of one of his soldiers. He did not dare hail the watchman on guard.

The woman had entered disguised as a boy and it was crucial she leave that way. If she was demented, he risked her crying out if he attempted to impede her speech.

Being a practical man, he saw he had no choice but to listen.

He looked at her more closely. She had fair skin, clear gray eyes with a hint of hazel.

He had never seen such eyes before.

He tried to keep his mind on her words. That proved not to be difficult for what she said made a great deal of sense if her information was accurate.

When she had finished speaking, he told her as much.

"I am not a British spy," she declared. "I have a small drawing of my husband that I carry with me."

She unfolded a piece of paper.

"I realize you probably don't know my husband. But you could take this paper and show it around and locate him."

Despite the fold line that ran down the center of the man's face, Leshoward recognized the private she claimed as her husband.

Ronald Leshoward had a good memory for faces. The countenances of the men, most of them mere boys as this one was, remained in his memory in detail.

I know my men far better than you could imagine, he thought.

"If you are not a British spy or a loyalist in the action of betraying your cause, how do you know all of this?" he asked.

She hesitated. It was a risk but she had faith in the truth.

"It came to me in a dream, the basic premise that your information about the enemy was reversed. I rose from my bed and dressed. Then knelt in prayer. That's when the plan to ward off this threat came to me."

"Madam. That sounds like witchcraft."

"No certainly not."

"Papist? A Catholic?" He recalled the story of Joan of Arc from his history class. A class taught from the British point of view.

"No. General, I am a Presbyterian."

"Like myself," he said thoughtfully. This woman was only giving him advice. Not trying to take arms herself. He was at a loss. "Now we are far past the 1600s, beyond magic and sorcery, into the rational, enlightened world of 1777. So how am I to take this?"

"Neither religion or magic enters into this. It is strictly a matter of military strategy."

"Perhaps you are correct. But it is a legal matter. Witchcraft is outlawed. By authority of- " He broke off, almost saying Parliament.

"You are surely the authority of this situation. Have me arrested. Try me for sorcery. I am a respected member of my congregation of my church and many will stand up for my piousness. So accuse me. But don't do it until after the battle. Take my advice and act on it. Follow my plan and then if you are victorious you will have more evidence against me."

"If I follow your plan and I'm victorious, I'm going to want to take you with me to the next battle."

"I'm sure we will never see each other again after tonight." The woman began arranging her hair and re-cloaking herself in the gender concealing clothing.

"You're leaving now?"

"I've done what my conscience dictated."

Leshoward stood up and somehow found himself within inches of the hooded woman. He looked down into her eyes and her face rose up to his.

"I could make inquiries as to which tent your husband is in and you could have a brief moment with him."

It took all the discipline the general possessed to keep his arms at his side as he spoke those words.

The face of the woman before him twisted slightly into a look of worried anticipation. For a brief moment Leshoward saw her age 10 years, glimpsed how she would look in a decade when she had passed her teens, borne her children, and journeyed past her 20s.

The tense lines vanished and her youthful glow returned. She shook her head slightly.

"It would cause attention to be brought to me. My visit would risk becoming a scandal. Let me just slip out as I came in. My husband and I said our fare-thee-wells when he departed. I am certain no harm will come to him. I have prayed incessantly for his safety."

"I will give you a pass this time. If you are stopped by the sentry there won't be any trouble," Leshoward said in a practical moment.

He quickly took his quill and scratched out a messenger's pass on a piece of scrap parchment.

She took it, folded it, put it together with the picture drawing of her husband, and hid it inside her robe.

Leshoward had a sudden pang, and irrational jealousy of the parchment that found a safe secure space within her bosom.

Then he thought of his wife.

And her ravaged breast.

Tears filled his eyes.

"Go carefully." He coughed and turned away.

"I've not far to travel and a good strong horse," she said, after a moment when he did not immediately continue. "I'm sheltering with other army wives safely behind the lines."

He faced her again.

"I promise I will give good consideration to what you said. Bear in mind whether you are right or wrong, whether I take your advice or not, when you hear the results of the battle tomorrow of the next day, take no blame upon yourself. It is my decision alone."

"I will take no blame for neither loss nor credit if there is a victory," she said simply.

He bowed slightly.

She curtsied, turned quickly, and left the tent.

He sat down at the table, realizing for the first time the ache in his legs from the continuous pacing.

He stared at the maps.

Prayers flitted, bidden and unbidden through his mind, interwoven with battle plans.

Three hours later, the snowstorm was worse. The winds were howling and there was nothing less than a blizzard on the outside.

The sentry on guard outside the tent was summoned.

A short time later General Leshoward, standing up, again placed himself at the head of the table full of maps and looked at his three subordinate field commanders at the other end who had been awakened from their pre-battle sleep.

"Gentlemen," he said, raising a pointer and reaching across the table. "There's going to be a change in plan…"

Fifteen years later...
1792

Chapter 1

A Weaving Mistress, dressed in the long blue robe and disguising veil that marked her trade, had almost reached the main road to the village when she heard a familiar horse making noises in the bushes.

"I cannot go that way," she whispered to her own horse.

The animal replied with a soft neigh.

"We have to go back. The watchman is following us."

She turned her horse onto the nearest side trail. It led back into the depths of the Kentucky woods. She and her kind had to travel at night.

It was dangerous. But she was unafraid.

She felt strong in her cause. And the dagger enveloped in the folds of her robe gave her confidence.

She veered off onto a small trail, a hidden pathway circling the woods but still leading to town.

She necessarily passed a cottage on the way and lights inside alarmed her.

The Weaving Mistress came to an abrupt halt before a small log cabin.

She dismounted slowly and cautiously.

"Fabric, are you in there? I know you are and who's with you."

It was a guess.

But she was right.

Fabric stepped out of the front doorway. He was shirtless despite the cold night air. His dark muscular chest broke out in chill bumps and he could feel the hair on his arms stand up as he rubbed them to try to keep warm.

He stepped outside rather than go back in.

"What's going on? Another one of those meetings? I see you are wearing the costume."

"Fabric, I know Emilia's in there with you. She has got to come with me. I have an extra robe. If anybody has seen her leave, then it can be said she was coming to join us. Far better for her to be branded as a Weaving Mistress than be caught with a slave."

"It was so cold tonight we had to use the cabin."

"Never mind about the cabin. Let's just get her out of here. I was being followed by my usual shadower. I shook him off but I don't know for how long."

A petite dark girl with olive skin and large dark eyes came into the doorway. She was dressed in thin cotton and she also shivered as the cold air hit her.

The woman pulled a robe from her saddlebag and tossed it at the girl.

The blue robe was synonymous with a permission slip to be out after the nighttime curfew in the new township of Leverageton.

"Emilia, put that on quick. Fabric, help her get on this horse with me."

"Will we be going to a meeting?" asked the girl, as they rode away from the cabin.

"We will pass right by the Mannstein estate. I will take you to the back door first. That's as far as I can take you."

"Yes, ma'am."

The younger girl had her arms around the waist of the older woman as the horse trotted away.

"I can't take you back inside the fort. The fort gates are being watched. Can you get home from the Mannstein estate?"

"Yes, I have a friend there. Naomi, the house servant. I can borrow a horse, get to the fort gates, and send it back by itself. But I wouldn't mind going to the meeting with you. I have been curious."

"I would take you but there is no meeting tonight. I'm out on other errands. I didn't want Fabric to know. He'd want to help and just get himself in trouble."

The rider dropped off her passenger at the back of the estate, crossed the pasture and emerged at the front, which was adjacent to the stone walls of the fort.

She knew the watchman would probably pick her up again.

As soon as she came onto the main road, she heard hoof beats behind her. She decided not to bother losing him again. The robe gave her the right to be on the street. So what if he knew where she went?

So long as he did not find out why.

A scrap of moonlight beamed.

She turned.

This time she had a clear look and she caught her breath in fear.

She had told her companion wrong. This was not the watchman.

It was a sister Weaving Mistress.

Sister in name only.

It was too late to veer away. There was little she could do but proceed to town.

The streets were deserted. There was a curfew that few ever broke. And because so few violated, they were rarely caught.

She stopped at a small corner building, dismounted, and tied up her horse.

The larger horse that had been following her had just reached the stopping point when she turned the door handle.

"Stop! I know what you are going to do. You have fake lists that you're going to substitute."

This rider was quicker to dismount from her horse. But she stumbled and fell.

"Mistress," called out the woman on the ground. She was shorter and lighter than the other, but lacking a defined profile. "Stop."

The taller woman ignored her and continued to strive to get the lock to work.

"Nonsense. I have no lists."

The shorter woman struggled to her feet. "Witch! I shall denounce you!"

"Who are you to accuse me? You are the witch."

The taller Mistress had just gotten the door open when her sister Weaving Mistress reached her.

"Witch," she said in a hoarse whisper. "You have betrayed us."

The taller woman clutched the knife she held beneath her robe and drew a sharp breath.

The shorter woman pushed them both through the doorway and drew a gun from her robe in a singular motion.

"You dare not shoot me," said the taller woman, as she allowed herself to be maneuvered inside the building.

13

"I will shoot."

The shorter woman stepped back, preparing the pistol.

"Very well. I have the documents within my robe." The taller woman spoke calmly, tightening her grip on the knife.

With her left arm, she pulled a parchment paper from inside her garment, as her right arm raised the dagger from beneath the folds of the robe. She whirled around and plunged at the other woman, knocking the gun from her hand.

After a short silence, there was a short moan, then silence again.

The knife was cleaned. It now had a companion weapon.

Blade and pistol were both pocketed within the robe of the taller woman.

The other stretched out in stillness on her back on the floor.

The ambulatory Mistress opened a secret compartment in the desk and extracted a list of patriots who had served the revolution.

Served behind the scenes, unknown to their friends and families.

She placed the parchments side by side on the table. A list of patriots. A list of loyalists.

All had served in secret, the odd ones out in their families and social circles, unsuspected to the end.

A third list- the one she had brought with her- she unrolled and compared to the longer documents.

This was a double column document containing the names of famous people, both contemporary to the 1700s and from the ancient world.

It was a list of characters for the upcoming gala and the names of those citizens who had won the lottery to portray them.

Besides these appellations were several names on the first two lists, which had been duplicated onto the third list and carefully matched to the famous characters.

Tonight's duel necessitated that this document had to be redone.

The Weaving Mistress settled down to a long time at the desk. She had to re-copy the entire parchment just to change a few names.

She became so absorbed in her work that she even forgot about the figure on the floor just a few short feet away.

Then a sound sent a chill through her.

The other woman was not dead.

Regaining consciousness, the injured woman was speaking.

The writer abandoned her work and knelt beside her victim, trying not to panic.

She had a simple plan for disposing of the body. But a living person would be trouble.

There might be a decision to make.

"Don't touch me!"

The wounded woman was talking clearly but remaining very still. Her voice was even toned and monotonous.

"I'm just trying to see what I can do for you."

"You have killed me. I know I am dying but I feel no pain. I have been lying here a long time knowing what you were doing. But it won't do you any good. My cause will triumph. The lists have already been changed."

"No pain?" The kneeling woman moved to take the other's hand.

"Don't touch me!" She panted a little. Bringing emotion into her voice was a tremendous effort.

"I would not have hurt you but you would have killed me."

"I feel great heaviness." She no longer looked at her attacker but at the ceiling, dimly visible in the lamp light. "I feel such heaviness. I cannot move."

"I will get some help."

"That is how I know. Many times, I have seen it in the animals just before the end. They make their sounds normally just like I speak to you now. But they cannot move. And they show no pain. I often wondered if they felt pleasure. But no, there is nothing. Just heaviness."

"I will go to get help."

But no move was made.

The stakes were so high.

Lives could be lost. Many good lives instead of one bad.

The injured woman began to pant and her eyes fixated on the ceiling.

It was now possible to check the stricken woman's wound.

It was dead center in her waist, looking to be through and through.

"You feel no pain?" There was no emotion behind the question. Just an attempt to get attention again.

"No- no- pain." She had to strain now to talk and words came in one syllable with a pause between. "The false lists!"

"What false lists?"

"Oh no! NO! God! There is pain now!" The dying woman screamed and tried to sit up. She groaned.

"I'll get help."

One had risen to her feet but the other had fallen back silent.

It was too late.

The wounded woman was dead.

Emilia was at last emerging from the woods headed towards the fort gates. It had taken a little time for Naomi to be able to help her get away unobserved.

She was on her way home now.

She had taken a shortcut through the Mannstein pasture.

She wound up on the same path her benefactor had been forced to take initially.

Oblivious of each other now, they were both being watched.

The watchman had not worried when his target veered off into the woods and he was unable to immediately locate her.

He knew where she had to emerge if she were going to complete her journey.

When Emilia came into view, he thought he had found his target again. He rode to intercept.

But at that instant, a different horse was coming down the road from town.

Distracted, the watchman turned his reigns when he saw waves of material fluttering in the moonlight.

Sure enough, the same distinctive outfit was emerging from a different direction.

This Weaving Mistress did not glance his way. She had to be aware of him.

As the stalker stood helpless, the Weaving Mistress left the road and disappeared in the woods.

It had been two different women. He was sure.

The one he was under orders to watch had gotten by him.

Or had he been bewitched into seeing the same woman coming from two different directions?

It was hard to see faces. The veils they wore covered almost everything except their eyes.

And with consternation, he comprehended he had tarried, trying to puzzle this out for too long.

He rode back to the gates of the fort.

He stopped at their barrier.

The second woman was gone also.

He had been tricked.

Meanwhile, the Weaving Mistress was deep into the woods and on her way home.

And Emilia was safe inside the fort.

Chapter 2

Emilia had managed to get back inside the fort so easily the night she had borrowed the robe that she decided it was worthwhile to use the garment again the next time.

The shortcut across the Mannstein estate also seemed worth repeating.

She had sent the horse to find his own way back to the estate the previous night.

The second night she was on foot from the beginning.

This time she was caught.

Private Crier, the soldier on patrol this night, decided she had to be one of the Mannstein servants, living in quarters on the estate, out after curfew without permission.

The private did not believe she was one of the Weaving Mistresses. She had the robe but it was excessively long for her and she had a foreign look about her.

The robe, a permission slip for night travel, was easily copied.

Only the nuns, Weaving Mistresses, and soldiers were allowed out after dark.

All distinguishable by their attire.

When the private brought Emilia to the house, Thistle Mannstein falsely identified her as employed there, thanked the soldier, and sent him on his way.

Inside the Mannstein house two people questioned Emilia.

"You're not one of us. Where did you get the robe?" Thistle Mannstein demanded.

"I was given the robe by friend to help me get away and not get caught."

Emilia was not too afraid.

The mistress of the house had not summoned the master, but instead summoned her servant, Naomi.

"Get caught doing what?" asked Thistle.

"Being with my man."

"You have a man? Which one? Do I know him?" Naomi asked.

"I cannot tell you," said Emilia.

18

"Wearing a robe that belongs to a group that you are not a part of for an illicit rendezvous with a man is a dire offense against us. If you are caught by the authorities it will cast suspicion that we are harlots and our robes are mere cover for sinful activities."

"I beg your pardon, Mistress."

"Who gave you the robe? If it was one of us, they are subject to extreme discipline," said Thistle.

"No one gave it to me. I stole it," said Emilia.

"You are lying. One story or the other. You borrowed it. You stole it. Both can't be true."

"In a way. I stole it from a friend. She didn't know. She won't mind. I was taking it back tonight."

"You're wearing it."

"So? Why should I be cold both ways when I can be warm on the first leg of my journey?"

"I am more inclined to believe you stole it than you borrowed it."

"I believe her, Mistress," said Naomi.

Thistle regarded Naomi with affection.

"Okay, I'll leave her to you. I will take the robe."

"Please just let me take the robe back. I haven't many friends. Don't ask me to betray her," said Emilia.

"It was a fellow servant who lent this to you," Thistle concluded. "Had to be. So it is of no matter to me. I can't spend all night debating this. My husband is waiting for me upstairs. He thinks I just came down to get a glass of cider and he's going to follow me down soon if I don't go back. Naomi, I'm going to leave this entirely in your hands."

"I am honored, Mistress," said Naomi. Though 19, she was little larger than a child, only her long thick blond hair had any substance to it. The rest of her was almost skeletal.

Thistle Mannstein tossed the robe on a chair.

"I trust you to make the right decision."

Naomi folded her arms and gazed upon her captive with satisfaction as her mistress left the room.

"See how my mistress trusts me. The robe makes us like equals.

19

Does your mistress trust you like that? She treat you like an equal?"

"All persons are not meant to be equal. It says so in the Bible."

"You are foolish. What you think we just fought this war for?"

"It was to make the white men equal with each other," said Emilia.

"No. We're all going to be equal. Even your man," said Naomi.

Emilia drew her breath sharply.

"I know who he must be. Who lives out in the woods besides the witch, Abigail Fichton, and Hayward Manchester? That slave."

"It is Hayward Manchester," Emilia said with a little bravado in her voice.

"Ridiculous!" Naomi scoffed.

"It is, I tell you!"

"Hayward Manchester wouldn't touch you. You are only one step above a slave."

"No. It's Hayward. He has many women. I'm just one of them."

"Doesn't matter. If you take a good look at him, he's not exactly all white himself. Although the other men treat him that way. I don't know why. But more likely it's that slave. I forget his name."

"Hayward Manchester is my lover," Emilia said stubbornly.

"I think you're lying. Listen, Emilia, we're both women, sisters under the skin. If we were both servants of the robe, you could tell me anything. We of the robe are cursed if we betray one another. Our limbs are severed from our body by a sword that has power all of its own."

"That sounds like nonsense."

Naomi stepped behind Emilia and put her arms on the other woman's hips. She tried another tactic.

"If you were part of us, you would not need a man."

Emilia pulled away sharply.

"We take care of each other," said Naomi defiantly. "Join us."

That argument did not work.

Emilia felt even more alienated.

"And you think it makes sense that I join in this group wearing a silly costume?"

"The garment is merely a robe to keep us warm. The veil keeps many from being persecuted by families, fathers and husbands who would beat them. Many hide from such men. Other women wear the veils to help them. So the men don't figure out who they are," said Naomi.

Emilia saw through this third attempt as well.

"I don't need to hide from anyone."

"Do you want to be a maide all of your life?"

"I love my mistress. Mistress Lantern's very sweet. General Leshoward is a kind master. I'm not their slave. I'm free to go at any time I want to."

"Then go ahead and stay with them. Join us and keep your identity secret. Like so many of us do."

"A secret? Even if I'm not in hiding or have no family to object."

"We have support in high places. You might could even get your nameless man some protection if they ever come for him."

Emilia's demeanor changed.

"There's powerful people who think we have the right to go about our business in peace," Naomi continued, her voice becoming more confident. "General Leshoward believes the group is an organization of war widows trying to earn money to live on. He has given us special privilege to wear our robes and go wherever we need at night so no one will persecute us as witches."

Emilia looked at Naomi with alarm. "Naomi! Are you a witch? It is said all over the township that you are all witches. I could not be part of your group. I'm not a witch!"

The other servant laughed. "I'm not in hiding and I have no family to object."

"Then what am I to believe?"

"We say we are war widows, and many are. It helps the group be more accepted by people who would otherwise not approve. Many keep their identity a secret because their husbands or fathers don't want it known they don't have enough to eat without the money they make."

"Do you make much money?"

"Yes! We sell our cloth for good prices. And without money there is no use in having freedom. But people turn up their noses at women trying to better themselves. Even their own families," said Naomi.

"I bet the families do not turn up their noses at the money these women earn," said Emilia thoughtfully.

She was seeing the group in a new light.

Chapter 3

Despite Emilia coming to serve for only part of the daylight hours, Lantern Leshoward was unused to being alone.

Until recently, her father was almost always there.

His duties were mainly administrative work from a small office in behind the staircase. The small contingent of soldiers was housed in barracks across the courtyard. There was a back entrance to his office for them.

Trials and justice were administered under the general's supervision.

No longer at the fort, however.

A new courthouse had been constructed on the other side of the township. With no civilian judge yet available, except by circuit travel for petty cases, the general had to make a day's journey to the bench.

As he had begun to do more frequently, he had taken the option of remaining overnight this time. He was getting older and same-day trips were harder.

The soldiers were just a walk away from the Leshoward home. There was thought to be little danger anyway as peace reigned in this section of Kentucky in the spring of 1792.

Still, Lantern was nervous.

It was unusual for there to be a knock at the front door at close to 11 PM.

Still awake and downstairs in the parlor, reading by the light of a dimly glowing fireplace, Lantern had a gun beside her chair.

As she opened the door, she was holding the weapon gingerly in front of her but then lowered it in surprise.

Her caller was a young woman.

"I've just arrived from Philadelphia. I'm looking for General Leshoward. You're not the servant usually here? You are too fair to be a servant," the visitor said hesitantly.

"I'm not a servant at all. I'm the general's daughter."

"I'm your cousin, Genevieve."

"So tell me about these women in business," said Genevieve, as she sipped tea.

"We are a colony of religious tolerance. Why not extend that tolerance to women?" Lantern asked.

After expressions of surprise and reserved delight upon establishing their respective identities, the two women sat in the large and friendly room.

Lantern lit the oil lamp and stoked the fire. The spacious room was soon bright and warm.

Tea prepared in the kitchen just behind the parlor made the new guest feel right at home, unleashing her talkative nature at once.

Lantern was not too surprised the Weaving Mistresses came up so quickly in the conversation. Often visitors to the colony were more curious about their organization than anything else.

So Lantern had a ready stream of replies to such comments.

"How do you see the two issues as connecting?" Her cousin countered Lantern's observation about tolerance with another question.

"If it's assumed that because a group of women get together and wear similar clothing and sell a product they make that they are witches, that assumption is religious intolerance," said Lantern.

"No one has taken any action against these women, have they? Either legal or otherwise?" asked Genevieve.

"Because it's very innocent. Perfectly harmless. It's a group of widows. Most of them had husbands killed in the war. They have children to feed. They need income. They have formed a company, making and selling cloth, giving the group a name," said Lantern.

"The Weaving Mistresses? Women openly in business is truly a new tenant of our democracy," said Genevieve. "I do most of my work in secret or, at least, quietly."

"Being a widow yourself, you should understand the need. Women are banding together to survive. There are no lawyers yet settled in the colony. So no one to profit by persecuting them."

"Indeed I do understand. If I didn't offer my services as a writer of pamphlets, letters, and essays, I would not eat."

"How do you make it? I know that, by law, widows can only inherit one third of their husband's property. I think for that reason, I shall never marry."

"I have my quill and ink. My horse and my clothes are my only possessions and my only expenses."

"You don't realize how often we speak of you and how we had hoped that you would come someday."

Genevieve stiffened. "Perhaps you don't know the whole story. I felt unwelcome for years."

The conversation paused abruptly.

During the ensuing silence, somewhat awkwardly Lantern retrieved the teacups and took them to the kitchen.

Lantern well recalled the story of her cousin's wedding. Genevieve had insisted on marrying a blacksmith, a man who later would serve with courage and give his life for the new country.

But at the time, Genevieve had been betrothed to Lantern's brother. Although he was a few years younger, being first cousins they were natural choices for spouses.

The broken betrothal had caused estrangement in the time before the war made the old customs obsolete.

Genevieve's parents later lost all their property during the war, then their lives.

Lantern had been a child at the time and remembered little of it. She knew her mother had died during the height of a crucial battle, which had gained General Leshoward a famous victory, making for a bittersweet triumph.

Lantern believed her father had never quite gotten over the disintegration of his home life and the advent of the changing society.

When Lantern returned, Genevieve was visibly more tense, rubbing her hands together.

"How did you travel alone all the way from Philadelphia?" Lantern asked, to break the silence.

"I had an acquaintance making the trip. She's quite well off with plenty of provisions. We rode the trail together."

"Oh, who is your friend?" Lantern asked.

"Actually not a friend. Ruthanne Webber. I don't know her. She was on her way to a horse farm about five hours on from here. I hope she makes it all right. It will be near 5 AM when she reaches the end of her journey."

"I don't think I know her."

"She is staying at the Melton estate. The families are friends. A betrothal is in negotiation for her after a long widowhood. Until the courtship begins she will be a companion to their daughter, Hortense."

"I do not know Hortense Melton," Lantern said slowly. "I do know her parents' estate is on the outer edges of the colony. They've quite a bit of land and numerous horses. They supply horses to the colony and thus are quite rich. But I hear, compared to ours, their house is quite small. Yet they keep slaves to tend it."

"You have a truly beautiful home. It is everything that my uncle described the one time he wrote offering me shelter."

"Where do you stay when you're not in residence working?" Lantern asked quickly, lest the conversation stall again.

"In Philadelphia there's a little room above a print shop. They let me stay there in return for service."

"It sounds like an exciting life."

"It is not. You have a more exciting life as the daughter of the general who governs this colony. "

"You have no idea how dull it is here. We are all excited about the first social event in ages. A gala celebrating impending statehood with someone important supposed to be coming from the east."

"I knew all about it in Philadelphia before I left. It's been talked about for weeks."

"Then you mean there might be something to the rumors that an important personage is coming?" Lantern asked. "I know this talk of imminent statehood has everybody buzzing. So perhaps a government official?"

"I don't know. All they care about in Philadelphia is land. What of the land my uncle was entitled to as a result of his war service?"

"He took far away acres to send Harkin to manage. My brother was too young to serve in the revolution but he is too old for the post war army. So sending him to manage the land at the outskirts of the republic fulfills his need to fight battles. Every so often he has to fend off renegade Indians, bandits, or die hard royalists. He keeps and maintains a force there and that takes most of the income from the land but sends us enough to live on."

"Far away?" said Genevieve. "So I suppose this means there's no chance that Harkin will come for the gala?"

"No, the journey would be several days. He would have already had to have started on his way," said Lantern. "Anyone not in the colony would have to be on their way already."

"I see," said Genevieve.

"I'm only asking this to make sure I understand how you feel. Would you want me to write Harkin and let him know you are here?"

Genevieve hesitated.

Her husband had been dead over a decade.

She was not yet 35.

"Not yet. You have much personal contact with Harkin?"

"We write occasionally. He disapproves of me continuing to be a single woman at my age."

"Then you are not close to him?"

"No, we are too far apart and different in many ways. Too many years between us."

"Then basically, we are both alone in the world. Although you have your father still. That will not be forever. I am also surprised you had no servants living here. You were completely alone when I arrived."

"Emilia is here ten hours a day. She lives across the courtyard near the barracks in a one-room building she shares with the soldiers' cook. The Continental Congress pays for no servant for us."

"I'm surprised my uncle stayed here at the fort with such a small contingent of soldiers. I hear the new government has very little money to pay them."

"My father supervised the movement of the original settlers from the fort into the town. They are still forming their city and he is acting as a governor for as long as they want him."

"And no formal militia?"

"The village men spend all their time keeping the roads clear and tending to the operations of the town, maintenance of the main street buildings. We have a print shop, tea parlor, and the general store. For a time, all able bodied men were members of the Fort Leverage militia. Father disbanded it. He believes an overloaded standing army invites conflict."

"So who keeps order?" Genevieve asked.

"There is a watch patrol directly under Major Plate's supervision. A soldier rides through the streets every night. There is little crime," Lantern assured her.

"So peace was declared in the 1780s with all possible enemies and a prosperous township is growing," Genevieve concluded.

"Right. The fort is really not needed anymore," said Lantern.

"Why not move out into the city yourselves?"

"As long as we stay here we get army stipends for food. The townspeople all have to work plots for their food. Father is not a farmer and likes the enclosure of the fort. And I love this house. I have freedom of movement throughout the colony. The fort gates are closed but rarely locked any more. The Penberthy and Mannstein estates are adjacent to the fort. They took the land next to the stone walls, forcing the village to locate nearer the river. Which is probably good for the township in the long run, Father says."

"So there are only two large estates so far?"

"Plus, the Melton horse farm, a day's ride."

"Yes, where my traveling companion was headed."

"I'm so glad you made the effort to travel here. And you do have a standing invitation to come here anytime and live. You would have freedom of movement also."

"Freedom of movement is overrated."

"On that we agree. I like staying home and tending to my sketches. I like to draw portraits. And I'm told I'm quite good but slow. I would love to have formal lessons so I want that freedom there just in case I need it."

"And you will marry. There's no question."

"I don't know about that. I hardly ever leave our compound."

"With the community still in process of building, I would think this is still the social hub of the colony."

"Not since all the colonials have moved out of the fort and started building the town," said Lantern with finality.

It crossed her mind that her cousin's questioning about the activities of the community was becoming repetitive.

Surely, there were other subjects to talk about.

Apparently not.

"Every building must be new in the township," Genevieve continued.

"There is an older section of buildings that make up the center of town. A print shop, even," Lantern said.

"Tell me more about this place with such interesting women who are so enterprising," Genevieve said.

"We have over 100 families in about 1.25 square miles. Many elderly couples and war widows. Most houses are new. And the reason many widows have homes of any kind is a result of their endeavors. That's why they have gotten together to make and sell cloth."

"I would think they are skirting with danger dressing up in identical robes. I know it seems like ancient history but in the overall course of human events the witchcraft trials were not that long ago. They are counting on our new freedoms to protect them from persecution. It's a tall order."

"As it was explained to me, they knew they would have to be out in all kinds of weather so they decided that they would get together and sew a large number of similar robes and they added headpieces to protect against the cold and rain."

"And what does my uncle think of them?"

"He has no quarrel with honest work. And he is impressed by their detailed organization. Plus, they revere the flag, sewing one for the fort for free. That makes him happy. So my father has requested they run the gala. He's giving them a chance to show they can be a valuable contribution to the community. Better they do the job than bringing in slaves."

Lantern hoped she could at least get the subject away from the township back to the gala.

That seemed to work, if the women's group was included in the conversation.

"So they are heavily involved. Why is the gala not being held at the fort?" asked Genevieve.

"The Mannstein home is larger than our house. It has a ballroom. The Mannsteins are not hosting the ball. Father is the host. That is his rightful place as leader of the colony."

"Are you the official hostess?"

"No, I am just a regular guest. I even purchased a lottery ticket to win a character. Everyone is hoping to win the right to portray a famous person. Weaving Mistress volunteers will make the costumes for the winners," said Lantern.

"It's a costume party?" asked Genevieve. "That was the rumor but I heard but-"

"Yes, a masquerade ball."

"The right to be one of these special personalities has to be purchased?"

"We are raising money for maintenance of the fort. Attendance is free. That is our only source of revenue."

"And will you have an escort?"

"Father will be my escort."

"Not the soldier whose mention brightened your eyes? Major Plate?"

"The regiment is providing security."

"So he will be there."

"Yes!" Lantern smiled.

"Mid-May. Only a short time away. It's not too late for me to come?"

"To try for a character, yes. But not to come. I can help you make an ancient world or peasant costume. Or one of the Weaving Mistresses will do it for pay. They are more skilled than I."

"Sounds interesting."

"Do come! We are hoping for out of town visitors. Richmond, Philadelphia, New York, even Europe."

"You do not think that is unrealistic?"

"Maybe. I don't care. I just want to have a good time," said Lantern. "So long as Major Plate attends, I will be happy."

Chapter 4

"I hear the King of Sweden is coming."

Thistle and her maide surveyed the wealthy woman's vast collection of dresses. Naomi chose one.

"To Kentucky?" Naomi asked with some surprise.

"Absurd rumors, I know. Then again, why not?"

"Surely he would go to New York to see General Washington, President Washington, I mean."

"Statehood is imminent. Perhaps the king desires to see the frontier." Thistle laughed.

"Fort Leverage is not exactly the frontier anymore."

"That's true. There would be no detriment to my being presented to him here in Kentucky. No anti-Catholicism to block me. He's quite enlightened. This king has revolutionized his country. It might be that he would come to Fort Leverage to see if the experiment in religious tolerance is working."

"I think it would be strange to have a king visit America. We just fought a war to get rid of the King. I would think people would not tolerate any royalty visiting here," Naomi said.

"Sweden is an ally of the United States. Like France. And the French are about to break the intolerant chains of monarchy. Speaking of tolerance, what decision did you come to about our intruder the other night?" Thistle said. "Did you report her?"

"No, Mrs. Mannstein. I recruited her."

"Excellent. The more people we have in our group spread out amongst the population, the more acceptable we will become. Now we have someone inside the fort. Leshoward has always been sympathetic to our stated cause. He is an enlightened man and feels women should have the structure to care for themselves that doesn't depend upon pity and charity. Naomi, I'm not sure. Perhaps I need to look at more than one dress."

As Naomi searched for another suitable gown, Thistle held up the first dress. "Never mind. I think this is going to be the right gown for tonight. I know it fits, so just lay it across the bed."

Naomi smiled as she rehung the other dresses. "Have you heard anything about your character?"

Thistle said, "I'm going to be Helen of Troy."

"No one would make a better great beauty than you," said Naomi.

"I hear my friend, Jane Penberthy, wants that character," said Thistle, smirking.

"From what I talk I have heard, Martha Washington would be more suitable for her."

"Yes, she does intend her husband to be president. That is the best she can hope for, though he would be king."

"She almost missed her chance is what I heard."

"Servant's gossip again."

"The soldier's cook told me all about how the general's aide was courting her."

"I advised her from the beginning she could do better than a major in the Continental Army. Little did I know she would take it to heart and marry the richest widower in this part of Kentucky. I only have myself to blame. I created my own rival."

A knock on the door disturbed their conversation.

Both women found weapons. It was the middle of the night and all of the other servants had gone to their own quarters separate from the house.

"Naomi, open the door. I will stay behind and dash upstairs to get my husband if it turns out to be anyone who's trying to cause trouble."

Naomi cautiously opened the door. Her fear was replaced by surprise.

"It's dangerous for you to come here, even at this time of night," said Thistle, stepping forward.

"I didn't have any choice. I need help."

Naomi and Thistle let the woman in.

She was wearing the familiar robe of the Weaving Mistresses.

Genevieve had found it easy to slip out of her uncle's house and beyond the fort gates. The detailed description of the colony and its surrounding area given by her younger cousin was a help.

She had several stops to make on her first night away from her kin.

The first was the print shop in town.

Later there was a rendezvous with a witch.

Even as she had ridden away, she had not worn the easily procured Weaving Mistress robe, but left it in her saddlebags. She had chosen it as a disguise over the nun's habit, which she also had.

For now, she did not want to be identified with either group.

It was a calculated gamble.

General Leshoward had not been completely successful in convincing the majority Protestant population that the convent was no threat to them. Nor had he completely managed to win them over to the idea that a group of independent entrepreneurial women were benign.

Although most citizens received candles from the nuns and cloth from the weavers when bountiful crops afforded the opportunity, resentment would occasionally surface, especially if prices rose.

Intolerance would mushroom overnight.

Free samples would then be proffered as peace offerings, easing tensions.

It was a fragile coexistence.

By traveling in her daydress, Genevieve risked a fine or a day in jail if she could not pay.

She did not worry. An envelope sewn into her dress pocket would take care of the situation if it arose.

She made it unobserved to town and easily slipped into the printer's shop.

She had a key to the shop and soon made herself at home in the empty structure. She found the papers she was looking for and got to work.

Chapter 5

The swing creaked gently in the moonlight.

The girl in the Weaving Mistress robe appeared to be asleep as the moving bench swayed lightly.

Two robed women stood holding each other as they watched the swing.

Another robed woman also stood watching and debating what to do.

Mistress Superior. The responsibility fell on her.

"When I got here I thought she was asleep. Then I shook her."

The swinging girl was dead.

"I thought surely she is out on this pleasant night, waiting for a friend, passing time, she's fallen asleep."

"And you are sure that is not the case? A deep sleep. Done with herbs perhaps?" asked the senior woman.

"Reach and touch her."

A reaction of horrific recoil put the swing in motion.

After that moment of shock, the ranking Mistress sprang into action abruptly. She grasped the dead woman by the shoulders and managed to pull her off the swing and down the porch steps.

"Help me, she must not be found here. We must get her hidden before any others get here. And much more has to be done."

They were able to get the body across the back of a horse. One had no choice but to mount with the corpse and hold her tight as the other led them away.

One remained behind to clean up and make sure no one else at the residence awoke and gave any type of alarm.

The two women and their burden were soon deep within the woods adjacent to the fort.

They scraped the earth with their hands until there was an indention in the ground, weeping as they positioned the body in a quickly dug shallow grave.

They raked dirt, branches, and small stones to form a coverlet.

The woman working at the corpse's feet appeared to finish first. But the Mistress Superior rose.

"Her face is uncovered," the kneeling woman protested.

"We must leave her thus," said the other, shaking the dirt off her clothing.

"We must leave her face uncovered?"

It was dark but there was moonlight. The two women could see each other's eyes.

The Mistress Superior pulled a long knife from her pocket.

"We must leave her face uncovered so the coyotes tear at that part of her first."

Without waiting for the others reply, she quickly knelt back down and cut open the cheeks of the dead woman. Then she raked the knife over her forehead.

The other turned away, weeping again.

"We cannot have it known who she was," said the Mistress Superior. "She is buried too shallow not to be found. The animals will tear her face beyond recognition. It will be their service to us."

"We must then say the chant for her," the other said.

"Not aloud."

"Aloud!"

"This is not that far from where there are occupied cabins."

"Aloud! Or I will make enough noise to rouse them."

"Okay. Calm down. We will say the chant," said the Mistress Superior, already planning ahead. "What we need is a diversion in the next few days. I have a couple of ideas. Oh, don't look at me like that. I know you think I am cold hearted."

"No," the other whimpered. "But I loved her!"

"So did I." The more practical woman pulled the other up from her knees. She grabbed her by the waist and kissed her.

"Now don't cry. Come, stand on that side of her and I will stand on this side." They reached their hands across the half-buried corpse. "Now just the short version. Speak softly."

Quietly, for they were cautious even when they knew they could not be overheard, when they were completely alone, they began to slowly chant.

A funeral chant, slow and mournful.

Chapter 6

Major Shears Plate was astounded to see a woman robed in a rather provocative shade of red coming into his office, which was adjacent to the soldiers' barracks on the opposite side of the courtyard from General Leshoward's home.

"Pardon me, Mistress," he said, rising. "I don't think we've met."

The lady in red turned, eyebrows raised. "I was looking for General Leshoward. A rather dark servant girl at his home sent me over here, saying he had not yet returned from a trip."

"That's right. The general isn't here. He's away right now and I'm in charge."

"I realize we haven't been introduced. Would you speak with me anyway? I am a widow. My husband served with the general in the war. He was killed at the height of the great victory."

"My sympathies," he said, with all the sincerity he could summon. He flushed and turned aside, his back partially to her.

Her expressive eyes surveyed him with suspicion.

"Who might you be? Please don't worry about formal introductions. I come from a Philadelphia area community. Proprieties are easily dispensed with now that the war is over."

He said, "My name is Major Plate. I am the second-in-command here at the fort. What can I do for you?"

He still did not turn to face her.

"Major Plate? I am Ruthanne Webber. Well then, there should be no problem. You heard I was coming, I'm sure."

"No, ma'am," he said.

Ruthanne was silent for a moment. Then she said. "You have never heard my name spoken by the general?"

"No, ma'am," he said, wondering silently why she expected him to know her name. "I do apologize."

She turned away from him in a dismissive fashion. "The command at the fort handles law and order for the colony?"

"Yes, ma'am. Exactly what part of the colony are you concerned with?"

"I'm visiting friends. The Meltons. I'm here to see you because

I'm concerned about their daughter, Hortense," said Ruthanne.

"Concerned? In what way?" asked Major Plate.

She cocked her head to one side. "I arrived at their home in the middle of the night last night to find myself greeted only by the elderly couple. While the Meltons tell me not to be troubled, I have to follow my conscience. I think she's missing."

Major Plate spun around, facing her. "Missing? What do her parents say?"

"They would like for me to believe she has gone to Philadelphia to visit friends. It makes no sense. She was expecting me to arrive to become her companion. Her parents are having a problem accepting the idea that something could've happened to her. So I rode back to consult with the general. I had been by the fort last night when I dropped the general's niece at his home. She was my traveling companion."

"I see. I didn't know anything about the general's niece coming."

"It was a surprise, I think. No matter about her. She is here safe and sound. It is my friend, Hortense Melton, I'm worried about. Can you possibly send someone back up the trail to inquire?"

"Certainly. We have couriers that leave almost every day and we receive communications at least five times a week. The postal system is just getting started in this part of the country but it's doing a good job. Can I offer you some tea?"

"Tea? I'm afraid I'll have to say no. I'm afraid I'm going to have to go. Those formalities will have to wait till later."

She gave him a sly look that he did not know what to make of.

He was disconcerted, looking away again.

"May I call on you as soon as I find out any information about your friend?" he asked.

"Yes," she said. "I will be looking forward to hearing from you soon under any circumstances. By the way, not that she is a friend of mine, but I have heard there is an herbalist living in the woods. Do you know anything about that? I have heard she is called Abigail Fichton?"

"I believe there is such a person. I have not met her personally. Fortunately, I enjoy excellent health. We don't have a doctor in Fort

Leverage yet. I understand she does a good trade," said Major Plate.

"Mrs. Melton told me she is a witch."

"Nonsense. Benign herbalism is permitted in the colony."

"Then rumors are true about a colony free from any type of religious persecution."

"Although I don't think Abigail Fichton calls herself a witch."

"I was just curious, that's all. Thinking perhaps she could help me find Hortense. I do have a miniature of her. I was going to take it to her but I can leave it with you instead."

"You have a miniature of your friend?"

Ruthanne hesitated. "I will leave it with you instead."

She handed Major Plate a small round portrait of a young blonde girl.

The fair girl was contrasted against the background of the American flag and wore dark blue clothing with a rather strange hat.

Still, her face was clearly drawn.

"I will do everything I can to find your friend. You won't need a witch."

Their eyes connected strongly as he let her out the door.

He followed to her horse and helped her mount.

She looked down at him for several seconds before riding towards the gates.

Chapter 7

"You are telling me you lost her? She tricked you with a double?"

General Leshoward had returned late from his short trip and gone straight to Major Plate's office for a report.

The small separate building that Major Plate used as an office also functioned as his quarters.

General Leshoward respected the major's free hours and did not bother him there at those times unless it was important.

The general considered Major Plate's surveillance of Abigail Fichton important.

The junior officer had no idea why.

"Obviously. Or maybe there were three of them. I'm not sure I was ever following the real Abigail Fichton at all. Remember, I have never seen this woman up close or in daylight. And they are now wearing those veils," Major Plate said defensively.

"Veils? What kind of veils? That is something new."

"Veils actually covering parts of their face so they won't be recognized. Similar to the Catholic nuns but not quite the same. They're not all wearing them. The story I was told is- there's been some harassment of some of the women who have joined this group so some of the later members have decided to try to be anonymous."

"How long is that been going on? I gave them latitude but some things are going too far. I guess I can always say it is to promote the gala, but if there are more complaints..."

"Am I the only one that sees this Weaving Mistress group as a perfect cover for theft or smuggling?" asked Major Plate.

"The group is gaining more and more acceptance in the colony. Congressman Craig's wife has joined," Leshoward said.

"She is not a widow."

"From what the congressman told me, they are now accepting substitutes."

"Substitutes?" asked Major Plate.

"It's a trial program. Mrs. Craig has taken on the position of a proxy worker. Everything she earns is going to an unfortunate widow who is physically unable to do any work. If it works, think of the benefit to impoverished invalids. Society ladies could step in, have a social outlet, and do good for their fellow human beings."

"If that is true, I could reconsider my opinion of the group."

"Henri Mannstein is making an open accusation of witchcraft," General Leshoward said worriedly.

"He's worried about witches? Where does he think he is? Salem in the 1600s?" Major Plate found it hard to take the wealthy landowner seriously.

"He's just trying to cause trouble. Yet he knows if we didn't let these women form a group and do their work, we would also have to deny the Catholic nuns their rights to live together and do their work."

"At least the Mistresses do not live separately from their families or society," Major Plate allowed.

"It is just going to take time for them to be accepted. And all this talk of witches is not helping. That is why I want you to keep an eye on Abigail Fichton. She doesn't hide behind any veil. She is an open target for those with the phobias of witches."

"It is the way she lives," the major said, wondering exactly what the word phobia meant but not wanting to seem ignorant by asking.

"There is more talk about Abigail Fichton living in the woods doing miracles with her herbs and potions than about any activities associated with the Weaving Mistresses," Leshoward said.

"What does Mannstein say about Abigail Fichton?"

"Mannstein claims that she is one of the Mistresses. He claims she is practicing religious witchcraft and he's threatening to bring charges against her," Leshoward said.

"Is she?" Plate asked.

"It is said that when she cared for a young girl in the midst of death throes the child inexplicably recovered," Leshoward said.

"That sounds like a miracle. He's Catholic. He should not be afraid of miracles."

"He is going to use the fact that she lives alone in the woods against her if it comes to a hearing," Leshoward said.

"Somebody needs to tell him this is Kentucky in 1792 and he's living in a colony that exercises religious freedom," said Major Plate, echoing his commander for the moment.

"Abigail Fichton does not call herself a witch," said Leshoward.

"Plus, she is not the only one living in a small cabin in the adjacent woods," said Plate.

"I would hope none of the women or our colony would be foolish enough to call themselves a witch but if they do, what am I expected to do about it? It is not a crime unless it's outside the boundary, actual devil worship," Leshoward said.

"Or, if it should affect the law and order and peace of the colony."

"No witchcraft is going to do that under my watch," Leshoward said.

"What exactly did he tell you?"

"He's actually suspicious that his wife has secretly joined with this mistress group and he is upset that she's adopted a cat."

"For heaven sakes. Maybe they have mice."

"If there's trouble between the Mannsteins, it is none of our affair. We're better off not knowing anything. We're striving for religious tolerance. Everyone knows we have Catholics and Lutherans. They are going to do strange things, probably. If we're going to practice toleration we have to leave them alone," General Leshoward said.

"Isn't that also a form of intolerance? Suppose this has nothing to do with Mannsteins being Catholic. I've heard the rumors that the wife sees other men."

"That is something we certainly don't want to know about."

"So what do you want me to do?"

"Maybe she is using this group to disguise her adultery. If so, we must not tell anybody. We don't want anything interfering with the gala."

"There is one person I would consult about this. Your daughter. I would like to spend a few hours conversing with her, if it is all right with the general."

"How will spending time with Lantern help you?"

"Lantern often has insightful thoughts and reacts with interesting interpretation of words I say to her. I value her

41

consultation."

"Major, that would sound suspiciously like sorcery to some people. Please don't tell me she sees the future," General Leshoward said.

"Certainly not. It is an intellectual talent, General. A very valuable one. It goes hand in hand with her talent as a portrait artist. It is natural and innocent. Given to her by the Almighty," said Major Plate.

"Go on then. I give my permission. What time will you spend with her? With what chaperon?"

"I would meet her publicly in the tea shop," Major Plate said.

"Very well, I give my permission. I will speak to the proprietor. He will keep an eye on you and deflect any gossip," Leshoward said.

"Thank you, sir," said Major Plate.

"I understand you have met Ruthanne Webber in a most informal way," said Leshoward.

"Yes, she was concerned about her friend not being here when she arrived. Due to her concern, formal introduction between us was dispensed with."

"What did you think of her?"

"A beautiful woman. Do you know her?"

"Her first husband was in my command. Killed in battle."

"Mrs. Webber also asked about Abigail Fichton. Apparently Mrs. Melton believes Abigail Fichton is clairvoyant and could help find Hortense."

"Nonsense. Mistress Hortense is capricious. Mrs. Melton is a terrible gossip."

"True."

"Would you think the idea of consulting a clairvoyant abnormal?"

"I don't know what I might do if someone I cared about was missing. I might look into every possible avenue."

"You're a good Protestant, Major Plate?"

Plate was used to sudden changes in the topic of conversation when he spoke at length with General Leshoward.

This one seemed a little more abrupt than usual.

At first.

"Well, yes sir. My family lives in Virginia. Do you need references for any reason?"

Happy thoughts of a promotion danced in Major Plate's head for a moment until the general dispelled that idea.

"I will need references for you to be able to court Mrs. Ruthanne Webber," Leshoward said.

"Court her?"

"It's time you married and settled down, Major. You obviously have ambitions within the army and our commander-in-chief prefers married officers. Your friendship with Jane Partington was looked at askance by some in society. But we are in a new country in a new age and should someone of her social stature fall in love with a soldier of honor such as yourself, especially considering the dearth of eligible young men following the war, it would be accepted."

"Thank you, sir," said Major Plate.

"But it wasn't meant to be, obviously. And you remaining single still? So near to her newly married to the possible next president of the United States- well it is simply prudent for you to marry also. You obviously like war widows and don't mind if your wife has a few years on you. Ruthanne Webber comes from a fine family. Impoverished by the war, they have died from diseases over the years and she is now alone in the world. Her husband's bravery in the battle that cost his life is undeniable. You could do no better."

Major Plate was astounded and it took all his concentration to not let it show.

He and Lantern had kept the depth of their friendship from her father, mainly because it had begun in true friendship and had not progressed much past that stage.

Yet he knew in his heart that she was expecting it to go forward to its natural conclusion.

He was the one that was unsure, so closely following his courting Jane Partington. Jane and the Leshowards were friends so that made it all the more awkward.

"You are serious?" Major Plate managed to say.

He took a good look at the general. Leshoward's face, somber and serious, said as much.

The general closed his eyes as he replied.

"I have also written to my son telling him the woman he was betrothed to many years ago has come back into my home where she belongs. So many people in the war are still alone after all these many years. What the war did to our social structure was unforeseen. There are war widows that have no children, such as my niece. Here, we have a shortage of young able men. Those of you too young for revolutionary service are just now coming of age. Our colony needs weddings and births to survive."

"To survive?"

"Time is running out," Leshoward said.

Chapter 8

The next day Major Plate decided it was a good idea to take another foray into the woods adjacent to the fort. The general was busy preparing for a political meeting and would not have need of him until it was over.

He was still looking for the witch called Abigail Fichton.

He did not think he was going to stumble across Hortense Melton.

He wanted to get a better feel for what was going on just outside the fort in the adjacent woods and on the Mannstein and Penberthy estates that were sandwiched between the fort and the growing township.

He felt unease from the beginning when the settlers started moving out of the fort to make the community into a town once the threat of the Indian subsided at the end of the last decade. He felt unease about people living alone surrounded by woods in a solitary environment that was difficult to access by horseback.

He knew that was how the supposed witch lived.

Although he had never met her, never having caught her at home during any of his expeditions.

It alleviated his suspicious nature that Hayward Manchester was almost always working in his spot.

Today Manchester was not there. But the major knew why.

The political meeting called many different kinds.

Plate frequently encountered another forest dweller, if the man was not off hunting.

No political meetings for him, no matter how open they claimed to be, Plate reflected.

This man kept to himself for good reason, coming out only when necessary for supplies, and to peddle a few furs occasionally to have money for those supplies.

He farmed a little plot next to a small cabin that he only took shelter in during extreme cold.

"This cabin is not mine," he had told Major Plate more than once.

"But you might could claim it as abandoned," Plate had replied each time.

But in his heart, he knew it was a futile idea. The man, known as Fabric, ran the risk that if he claimed the cabin someone would dispute that claim and claim him.

And there were others who came in the night to use the cabin. Persons Fabric wanted no part of and rightly feared would chattel him if he let them know he knew they met there.

Fabric was a slave.

Fabric had no legal rights. As a person, he did not exist. He was property with no owner.

This day Major Plate once again had no luck in finding Abigail Fichton. But Fabric was working away in the small plot of land adjacent to the cabin that had belonged to his owners, who had perished in the last flu epidemic.

"How can I help you, Major?"

The strong bronze skin man put his hoe against the tree and walked towards the soldier.

"I'm looking for a missing woman, Hortense Melton. Young, blonde. About 19 maybe."

"I've heard of no woman missing around here."

"Her parents wanted it kept quiet. They claim she's gone to Philadelphia. I think they fear she's run off with a man. They are Meltons of the horse farm on the outskirts of town. I know they have slaves. Do you hear anything from them?" asked Major Plate.

"I know about that farm. Never had any dealings with the folks. I don't expect you would think the girl would be out here with me?"

Major Plate laughed and Fabric joined him.

"No, I'm just grasping at straws, hoping I can find something out. Hoping actually to run into Abigail Fichton."

"Haven't seen her about no time recently. And she and I kind of keep in touch just to make sure the other's alive. But she does take off from time to time to go traveling."

"Dangerous for a witch to go traveling."

"She's never claimed she's a witch."

"I've never been one to pry. But some occurrences are

concerning me lately. What do you actually know about her?"

"She didn't become a witch on her own. That was done to her. I don't recall the details. She told me once when I think I'd had a little bit to drink. Had to do with the church. That's all I remember."

"Thanks, Fabric," said Major Plate.

"One more thing," said Fabric. "Last night I heard singing in the woods."

"Singing in the woods?" asked Major Plate.

"Yeah, you know chanting sort of. Kind of like the Catholics do."

"Could you tell where it came from?"

"No, Major. It was windy. But it was not in the cabin this time."

"Thanks for mentioning it, I'll look around."

"Might have been gypsies," suggested Fabric helpfully.

"None around here that I know of. You know you could actually stay in the house. Nobody would care."

"Thank you, Major Plate. But you and I both know somebody would decide to care. Long as I sleep out under the clouds, no one can get me."

Chapter 9

"I hear Thomas Jefferson is coming to the gala," said Father McKinsy.

"I fail to see how my being this character is going to work to our advantage," Hayward Manchester said to the small group of men seated with him at the tea parlor after hours.

They included Father McKinsy, the Reverend Falldrem, Reginald Penberthy, Henri Mannstein, General Leshoward, and Congressman Marchmont Craig.

"I think we're taking this masquerade ball way too seriously," said Craig.

"But if Jefferson actually comes?" Father McKinsy ventured.

"That's just a rumor. I heard one that the King of Sweden was coming. Another that we would be seeing the King of France," said Penberthy.

"Have you not heard the French are in chaos?" Craig asked.

"We don't care what goes on in Europe," said Falldrem.

"Thistle says they are trying to save the monarchy in France," said Mannstein.

"European aristocrats! Here in Kentucky!" Falldrem made a gesture of disgust.

"I wouldn't pay any attention to all of that. We need to be satisfied if the governor of Virginia comes. He has indicated he will support you, Reginald," said Leshoward.

"I am Lutheran. Too many have not forgotten the Hessians that fought for England against us," said Penberthy.

"I think that is nonsense," said General Leshoward. "Your religion is no barrier to you."

"Our problem is we have no one who is exactly right in every respect according to the trends in the country these days. We would need the right religion, the right age, the right birthplace, the right occupation, the right heritage. It's impossible," said Craig.

"We have Hayward here. Are you committed to a denomination, Hayward? I notice you rotate attending different churches in the colony. Settled on one yet? If not, we can have you pick the most acceptable to voters," said General Leshoward, his words not completely facetious.

"Me? I thought we were here to talk about this upcoming masquerade ball, not politics or religion."

The others laughed.

"I would not mind a move to the new senate," said Craig.

"You were not in the war. You are too young," Mannstein commented.

"Technically to run for president, but not senator," said Craig.

"Both senators from Kentucky cannot come from this colony," warned Penberthy. "And we don't have enough population to rate more than one congressman."

"And the obstacle for me is?" asked Reverend Falldrem.

"Your occupation. We need a man not of the cloth for this purpose," said Craig.

"The obstacle- " Hayward began.

"Your inexperience. The only obstacle for you is your inexperience," said Leshoward.

"The obstacle to my having the character I want at this ball," continued Hayward.

The other men all looked at Hayward again and laughed.

"I don't like the idea of this masquerade ball. There's something of paganism in dressing up in costumes of dead people," said Reverend Falldrem.

"The famous people we're dressing up as are very much alive. Thistle struck off Benjamin Franklin from the list when we found out about his passing," Mannstein said.

"What about Julius Caesar? I don't see how you can say Julius Caesar or Cleopatra or any of those people are appropriate role models that we should desire to dress up and pretend that we are them. And they are dead," Falldrem said.

"Those are the ancient world figures. That's different. You're perfectly at liberty not to attend the ball if you don't want to. The activities at the ball may not suit the religious ideals of all the denominations of the Christian faith. But we pay homage to religious freedom in this colony as long as I'm running it," said General

49

Leshoward. "Clergy wanting to come and build their churches here agreed to that condition. Is that not true?"

"Yes, I did," said Falldrem. "I had so many of my denomination coming here, I felt I had to compromise for them so they would have a church to attend. I am beginning to regret it. Aren't you, Aloysius?"

"The Holy Church goes wherever she is called, giving thanks for all circumstances," said Father McKinsy diplomatically.

"Is paying homage to the idea of religious freedom the reason why we allow those witches to roam the colonies selling their cloth? Now they're going to be running this masquerade ball?" asked Mannstein. "I am uneasy allowing them in my house."

Said General Leshoward, "The alternative is to bring in slaves. There's a servant shortage in this part of Kentucky. What would you rather have? A group of industrious women who are trying to make something of themselves in our new world? Or slave labor?"

"It would seem I don't know what is going on." said Hayward.

"Having just returned, I am still catching up on the latest news myself," Leshoward said.

"You must hate having to go beyond the town center to that new courthouse to pass judgments," Penberthy said.

"Necessary progress to our statehood and acceptance back east as social equals," Craig said.

"Sounds like a time consuming waste," Hayward said.

"The ball is a social event to introduce you and Reginald to the powerful people who are governing our new nation, who will be guiding us as we become a new state. We have been planning it for months. You're so involved in your work you need to come out from the blacksmith shop sometime. We have potential national leaders here, we are expecting a statesman to come from the east coast. I too have heard rumors it will be Thomas Jefferson. We mustn't get our hopes up. It may be a lesser personage," said the general.

"And the rumors about European royalty?" asked Hayward.

"Even you in your isolated shop have heard those rumors? We are trying to keep the gossips quiet about that. If the great statesman comes, he has a long journey. A lot of things could prevent him from arriving so therefore we are not making any announcements,"

Falldrem said.

"The least we are hoping is that this social event will get the attention of those in New York and Boston and Philadelphia and yield a national leader from our community here in Kentucky," concluded Penberthy.

"Our best hope for a national figure to come from Fort Leverage is you, Hayward," declared General Leshoward.

"I fail to see that," said Craig. "No offense, Mr. Manchester."

"No, none at all," said Hayward in a bewildered tone of voice. "This is all news to me."

"Hayward is a maverick and freethinker," said Leshoward.

"We need to build on tradition and stability," Craig said.

"Hayward's tough reputation will not hurt. He is already known beyond Kentucky for his sword making ability," Leshoward said.

"Did you kill, with a single one of your swords, 27 redcoats? And before you turned 16?" asked Father McKinsy. "That is the story I heard."

Hayward rolled his eyes.

"I am astounded at all of this, gentlemen. I am a mere blacksmith. I happen to make swords that others have judged to be exceptional. I have no political ambitions."

"Do you mind being here? Are you impervious to our cause?"

"I certainly do not mind. I am for Kentucky's cause. For Fort Leverage's cause," said Hayward.

"I can see where having influence with the new national government would be advantageous to the colony. This is going to be one of the strong areas of the nation. We have a bounty of natural resources, plenty of animals, horses, and cattle. Woods to harvest for homes. I don't see how we can lose," Penberthy said.

"We just have a shortage of men younger than 25 but older than 13. On the other hand we have a plethora of women that age plus a significant number of slightly older widows from the war. Many of them have children. But there is little new marriage and few new babies born," Leshoward said. "And we face a labor shortage. These days few are willing to act as servants or laborers."

"Surely the labor shortage can be solved by slavery," Craig said.

"I've been actively discouraging slavery in any significant numbers. I know we can't outlaw it. But if we can keep it to the one odd family that has a couple of slaves or these small enterprises that employ a few indentured servants and possibly a slave or two, we can keep slavery on a large scale out of our area," Leshoward said.

"Those plans are not going to work." Penberthy scowled.

"What are your feelings about slavery, Hayward?" asked Craig.

"Gentlemen, I assure you I'm not a political person. I won't say I don't have opinions on slavery but I'm not sure I'm qualified to express them," said Hayward.

"I think we can take that answer to mean that you're open-minded?" Leshoward asked.

"I think we can take that answer to mean he doesn't want to tell us how he feels," said Penberthy.

"It will all work to his advantage someday. Some of us see an unlimited future for him," said the general.

"But we have to work in the present," reminded Penberthy.

"At the present I feel like my position is being attacked," said Congressman Craig.

"Marchmont, we are merely looking beyond the time when General Washington will be no longer be president. And that's going to be soon," said Penberthy.

Hayward flushed.

"Congressman Craig does not want to step down. Mr. Penberthy plans to take the senate seat when statehood arrives. So what do I do?"

"Maybe it is not clear. But I am certain you, a Revolutionary War hero, with a most interesting ancestry, maker of swords sought all over the continent- there is a place for you among those who direct and guide our new nation," said General Leshoward.

"Our family folklore that my great-grandmother married a native Indian and that his ancestry somehow led to Asia is merely stories that have been passed down. There's no written documentation. No proof whatsoever. I admit my mother was a slight woman and her eyes did slant. Several medical conditions can cause that. I hardly look Asian," said Hayward.

"How then do you explain your sword making ability?" asked Mannstein.

"Has it ever occurred to any of you gentlemen that I worked very hard to become the skilled craftsman that I am? It had nothing to do with any ancestors. I will be frank. It is perhaps helpful in my business to allow a bit of mystique concerning samurai warriors to linger about the establishment."

"Beware of mystique, my son," said Reverend Falldrem.

"In what way?" asked Hayward.

"Mystique can be mistaken for witchcraft," said Mannstein.

"God also uses divine mysteries to accomplish His purposes," said Father McKinsy. "The devil does not have propriety over divine mystique."

"No one can escape their destiny," said Mannstein.

"We do need to talk sometime, Henri," said Father McKinsy.

"We may seem an odd team. We may seem often at odds. But we are all together in fact. Are you ready to join us?" asked the general.

"Yes," said Hayward.

"A good start for you in this social world, Mr. Manchester, will be for you to attend a dinner party tomorrow night at my home. Meet my wife. Congressman and Mrs. Craig will be there. I will tell Thistle to ask around among her lady friends and find a suitable companion to sit with you," said Mannstein.

"And my wife and I will be there," Penberthy said.

"And, General?"

"Alas, now I have to undertake a short journey tomorrow."

"I will be preparing for service and will not make it," said Reverend Falldrem.

Father McKinsy, not knowing if he was invited, remained diplomatically silent. He understood that Thistle Mannstein liked her parties populated by couples only and there was no way anyone could make a couple out of him.

"You are welcome at all times, Father," said Mannstein.

The priest bowed out diplomatically. He did not like to cross Mrs. Mannstein.

"Unfortunately, I cannot make it tomorrow night."

"Then surely I can expect you at the ball, at least," said Mannstein.

"I will most certainly be there, hopefully in a costume. I have entered the lottery, but not been notified yet. I have requested a certain one," said the priest.

"Then I should have the same privilege," said Hayward.

"Fine," said General Leshoward. "Which character was that?"

"Julius Caesar," said Hayward.

"Fine. Let me take this notification to the Mistresses and I'll get it changed. If the person who drew Caesar has already been notified, we will tell him it was a mistake and give him your character," Leshoward said. "Anyone object?"

No one did.

"I appreciate that, gentlemen," said Hayward. "You don't know how much it means to me. At least Caesar doesn't wear one of those white curled wigs."

The other men all laughed.

Chapter 10

Reverend Falldrem indicated to Marchmont Craig that he needed a word with him in private.

The two men remained behind as the others left.

"This will only take a second," said the reverend. "And I hate to have to put it this way. It's about your wife. Well, there have been some complaints. I know she's been in the group a long time but now that the colony is growing, we have new people coming into the congregation who are really talented…"

Leshoward took Hayward by the arm as they left the building.

"Did you want a word, General?"

"Yes, too many people live alone in this colony. Man is meant to be with woman," Leshoward said.

Hayward's eyebrows rose.

"I am satisfied and content in my blacksmith shop. My house at the edge of the woods is small but I spend little time there. Only to eat and sleep. I work most of the daylight hours," Hayward said.

"You must soon be a rich man. I hear you only accept coinage, silver and gold."

"I have little time to spend my profits."

"A wife would also help you in that respect," Leshoward said.

The general and the blacksmith both laughed.

"Have you someone in mind? Not many mistresses in this colony are interested in me. The discrepancy in my ancestry puts them all off. They fear the savage Indian blood rising up in their children."

"I know one mistress who would not have such prejudices."

"Indeed?"

"Indeed, for I raised her myself. My daughter, Lantern."

"Lantern? I admit I'm surprised. I did hear you had an eligible daughter. I am almost 40. You would want me for a son-in-law?"

"I believe you are destined for great things."

"I have not ever given marriage much thought. Your daughter? She's little more than a child, isn't she?"

"No, much more. She runs my household with only a single day servant. She's intelligent. I educated her. She reads and writes well. She has a quick mind which is open to intellectual thought and kindness. I believe she is well grounded in her religion. And she would make any man a good wife," Leshoward said.

"I hear a qualification to this," Hayward said.

"Only that she is the most dearest person to me in the world and I don't want her taken from Fort Leverage."

"And if those great things I am destined for take me from Fort Leverage?"

"She can make her home here while you go off to pursue your greatness. That's a common situation in our day and time."

"And the benefits to me?"

"Not much I admit. My lands are willed to my son. He will undoubtedly marry and start his own family. I have an orphaned niece whom I must provide for if she refuses to marry my son. So I cannot offer much of a dowry. Mostly I can offer myself as your father-in-law. I am a general. I have some connections back east that will benefit you. And there is the value within Lantern herself."

"And how does Lantern feel about marrying me?"

"I have not approached her with the idea."

"I see. You wish me to begin a courtship?"

"Are you adverse to that idea?"

"Not at all. I do want to seek the advice of the other men who have been speaking with me lately about my future," Hayward said.

"That's most understandable."

"And I would want Lantern to be amenable to the idea."

"Wonderful. Why don't you send a message to Lantern asking her to attend the Mannstein dinner party tomorrow night? The girl never goes anywhere, has virtually no social life at the fort, and I'm and sure she would love to go with you," said the general.

"Thank you. I was dreading whoever they might come up with being a real witch."

The smile Hayward expected this remark to produce failed to appear on the general's countenance.

Chapter 11

Hayward Manchester arrived slightly late and solo at the Mannsteins. By messenger, he had invited her, and by messenger, Lantern Leshoward had refused his invitation to come as his guest.

It was too late to inform the Mannsteins to have another suitable eligible woman take her place.

But Hayward was more concerned about being late than alone.

Both social sins were overlooked by his host and hostess.

However, he felt hostility from the Craig couple that had not been evident before. The experience made him tired, a feeling strange to him except in satisfaction at the accomplishments of his hands.

So when Thistle Mannstein outlined a game of sophisticated hide and seek, he declined and left. The objective of the game- to find a member of the opposite sex alone while other players were redirected to a dead-end location- seemed extremely juvenile to him.

It would have been more interesting if follow through of sexual innuendo were permitted. But merely finding someone alone who could potentially be a sexual partner was the climax of the game. Naughty in nature, it had resulted in several betrothals since it had become popular.

Hayward's departure left only Thistle's husband and the other guests, Jane and Reginald Penberthy, Marchmont and Margaret Craig, and the maid, Naomi- the other servants having retired to their separate quarters for the evening after the meal- on the premises when Thistle Mannstein disappeared.

At the precise time she disappeared, Thistle Mannstein was alone in her husband's library save for her solid black cat, whose green and yellow eyes were visible in the dark through the door's small window.

Sorcery was seen as the only explanation.

After searching the entire house as part of the game, Marchmont Craig glimpsed Thistle going into the room. He tried to follow her but the door was locked, prohibiting him from declaring victory and claiming his embrace.

Angrily, Henri Mannstein had loudly called the game off.

Thistle was behaving like a child. She couldn't stand to lose.

The group gathered in front of the door. Through its small window only a large desk was visible. A flickering candle was threatening to flame out, leaving the room in complete darkness.

"I'm worried that Thistle is not answering me," said Mannstein. "We can only see a limited section of the room and she may have fainted or become ill in a corner where she is not visible."

Everyone took turns calling for Thistle for several minutes. There was no reply except a meow.

Reginald Penberthy and the Craigs looked at each other uncomfortably.

"I think we should open the door. Or maybe I can go around the side and wedge myself through the window. If someone will give me a boost, I might could get my fingers in between the sashes and flip the lock," said Margaret Craig. Muscular for a woman, Margaret was tall and thin, with long limbs and long spindly fingers.

"Absolutely not," said Marchmont Craig. "I won't have you taking any risks right now."

Margaret smiled slightly. "Not a risk yet." She patted her lower abdomen, the only part of her body where any excess fat resided. It was protruding a tiny bit.

The congressman put his arm around her.

A hint of smoke and the demise of the flame got their attention.

The group was startled by the clear sound of a giggle from the now completely dark locked room.

"Thistle, this is not funny!" said Mannstein angrily. "I'm opening this door. I am getting my key."

After a short search, Mannstein located a key in the pantry. Mannstein pushed the key into the lock that held the door in place, and turned the cylinder.

He and Jane each pushed on the door at the same time.

Naomi materialized behind them and lit candles on the table.

The feline flew out.

Thistle Mannstein was nowhere to be found.

Chapter 12

Still dark, it was now early hours of the morning. Major Plate had spoken to the guests, the housemaid, and the husband. Guests having departed, he turned once again to the latter two witnesses.

Mannstein was still proclaiming his wife had vanished into thin air.

The major disdained witchcraft as an explanation for the disappearance of a human being.

"You mean you saw her last in this room?" asked Major Plate.

"I saw her last in this room. We all did. And she never left it."

"Then, behind these curtains?" The major put his hand on a hanging satin panel.

"Behind one curtain is a dressing area. Behind the other is a window."

"Then it is perfectly simple-" Naomi began.

"Then she went out the window," Plate interrupted.

"Impossible! She couldn't possibly have gone out the window without someone noticing. The curtain was untouched. Nothing was disturbed," protested Mannstein.

The Major frowned. This was shaping up to be more than just melodramatic adult games or witchcraft.

"No one else went into the room with her?" Major Plate asked.

"No. No. Well, her cat followed her in. Damn cat follows her everywhere. Black devil."

Major Plate had to put one more suspicion to rest.

The only drink allowed in the colony was the wine for the Catholic Church Mass.

"Perhaps did Father McKinsy visit that afternoon?" asked Major Plate.

"No. And I resent that insinuation. Thistle would never allow wine intended for Mass to be used for entertainment," said Mannstein.

"I apologize, I meant no disrespect. But I have to explore all possibilities. I do know something of her background which has little provenance and some ambiguity," said Plate as politely as he could manage.

59

"It is true she was an orphan. Then she married a Protestant who died in the war. She hid her Catholicism, understandably. She declared she was of the true faith when I started paying her court. There was not one daring to dispute her. She knew the Latin Mass by heart," said Mannstein haughtily.

Major Plate was impatient that he had been misunderstood.

"I do apologize. My point is that while the colony laws require total abstinence from alcohol, we know that wine is sometimes overlooked. And legally no one is allowed to import it except the priest."

"There was no alcohol at the party!" said Mannstein.

"You've had no contact with the herbalist, Abigail Fichton?" asked Major Plate.

"Certainly not! The woman is a witch! She dare not enter my home."

Naomi asked if she could retire for the night.

"If I could ask you one more question," said Major Plate. "About the Weaving Mistresses. A watchman saw one coming across your lands. Did she stop her or was she trespassing?"

Naomi hesitated.

She did not want to betray a friend.

Major Plate nodded slightly to Mannstein who discreetly left the room.

"There was one of them come here asking for help," Naomi said. "She claimed she had been attacked in the woods. I cleaned her up a little and sent her on her way."

"Do you know the identity of this woman," asked Major Plate.

"It was the witch, Abigail Fichton," said Naomi.

Chapter 13

"Did your wife have any connection at all with the Weaving Mistresses?"

Major Plate gazed across his desk at the simply dressed man nervously twisting his fingers as he reported the disappearance of his wife.

The husband was explaining he knew little about his spouse.

"My first wife died three years ago. I have two small children needing a mother," said Neilman Horaceton.

"Then you have not been married long?" asked Major Plate.

"Prudence and I married about 10 months ago."

"She was a war widow?"

"No, not exactly. Her husband was a man who had injuries left from conflict. The famous victory General Leshoward won. He died of long-term complications just two years ago."

"I see," said Major Plate. "So about the Weaving Mistresses?"

"It's funny you should ask that. I was hoping they would open up their ranks to non-widows. We could use a little bit of extra, even if she just got paid in cloth. But she was leery. Said she had heard witchcraft was involved."

"Yes, just rumors," said Major Plate. "No proof. Had you gotten any response to your request for her to join them?"

"I found out they were only accepting women of society who were willing to donate all of their earnings to invalid widows. Prudence did not qualify."

"I don't understand that type of thinking," said Major Plate.

"Do you think they can have some type of connection to her disappearance? Surely they're not really witches?" asked Horaceton.

"I'm afraid I don't know much about witches," said Major Plate. "This group does seem to be making quite a bit of money."

"I would say you are correct about that. They have finer horses than I could ever afford."

"They are the only consistent source of cloth in the colony. The traveling peddlers rarely have enough quality stock and the eastern arrivals at the general store are still unpredictable."

"I am only a poorly paid schoolmaster. We don't have a lot of extra money to buy cloth. She was even making her own costume."

"Costume? You are attending the gala?" asked Major Plate.

"She's been talking of nothing for weeks but this masquerade ball. She had her heart set on attending. She left home for a routine trip back up the wilderness trail to get some supplies. She left April 13 and I was expecting her back in three days."

"Was she traveling alone?"

"No, she went with a group from the colony. With one or two exceptions, they've all come back but she did not. They said she started back with them but somewhere along the line they lost her. I've only talked to one or two of them. Most of them are scattered about the colony and I haven't been able to track them down."

"Can you give me the names of the people that you know she left with, the ones that have come back? I will try to talk to those people to see if they say anything different."

Neilman Horaceton relayed a list of names to Major Plate. Most of the people would be easily found within the colony although tracking them all down would be time-consuming.

One person Major Plate was afraid he was not going to be able to find.

Abigail Fichton.

Chapter 14

Emilia was at the home of General Leshoward to open the door to Hayward Manchester.

Hayward was impressed by the size and elegance of the general's home. Being located inside the huge, nearly empty fort, it looked small in comparison. But it was spacious inside with all the required rooms for an upper class southern mansion, even if the décor was much more Kentuckian than Virginian.

Emilia curtsied to him and showed him to the front parlor, explaining Mistress Lantern would soon be greeting him.

"Hayward Manchester?"

Hayward turned to see a thin and willowy woman with green eyes and light brown hair, which could easily be mistaken for blonde in bright sunlight.

He was a hardened warrior, master swordsman, and solitary worker.

He was shaken that blood could rush so fast through his veins at the sight of a woman.

"Mistress." He bowed. "At your service."

"The general sent you here?"

"I thought I was expected."

"He tell you why?"

"For us to get to know each other," Hayward said.

"The general does have his practical side. It tends to rear its head at the most inconvenient moments."

"May I say that, having seen you, I have no adverse thoughts against any of his proposals."

"You might reconsider that idea when you take a look at his proposals in depth."

Lantern entered the room that moment a little breathless.

"I see you've greeted our guest, Genevieve. You must be Hayward Manchester." Lantern gave a little curtsy. "I'm Lantern Leshoward. I'm sorry our introduction couldn't have been more formal. My father had to leave on business again."

Hayward could not keep the surprise from his face. He looked with astonishment at Genevieve.

"I'm Mrs. Genevieve Brown, the general's niece. I'm here on a short visit from Philadelphia."

"My apologies. He didn't warn me- er, tell me that you were here. Of course, you are to act as chaperon," Hayward said.

"Certainly I am qualified. I am years older than Lantern and a widow."

"I must say you certainly do not look any older. I was aware of Mistress Lantern's age and gave no thought but that you were her when I first saw you."

After Hayward Manchester had spent an hour chatting with the two cousins, Lantern excused herself and went upstairs.

For the rest of the visit neither Hayward nor Genevieve missed her at all.

Chapter 15

"So you're going to be chaperoning me and Hayward? I think it's turning out to be the other way around."

Lantern giggled a little as she spoke.

"I did appreciate your perception in going upstairs. He bedazzled me. I've given no other thought to no other man but my husband these past many years," said Genevieve.

"Admit it. You've kept away from us all these years because you thought sure my father was going to match you up with Harkin again. Now that Harkin's far away, you feel like you're safe."

"I did. I did feel safe. Now I've come back just in time for another scandal. How is he going to react if I steal your fiancé away from you?" Genevieve asked.

"I no more want Hayward Manchester that I want a grizzly bear. But don't feel too safe yourself. Father told me he has sent for Harkin, telling him you were back," Lantern said.

"I see no future in my position with your father. First, I jilted his son to marry another man. Then I will take the man he wants to marry his daughter. And make no mistake, I will take him."

"I shall be most grateful if you do not tarry."

"Are you still stuck on your soldier?" Genevieve asked.

"Never mind about me. Deep in his heart, Father would not mind so much if I remain single. I could live with that idea also. Father only fears my being left alone when he dies. If you were to marry Hayward Manchester, and your husband does become an important politician, then I would have relatives to care for me."

"Sounds like a good plan to me."

A knock at the door interrupted this budding conspiracy.

The news that a body had been found in the woods put a chill on the anticipations of the Leshoward cousins.

A messenger soldier brought the news in the form of a verbal communique as he also delivered an unrelated parchment.

Fabric had discovered a body beneath leaves near his plot, the soldier informed the women, though the message was officially for the absent men.

Permission had been given by Father McKinsy so the unknown had been taken to the convent where the nuns were caring for it in hopes of discovering the identity before burial became imperative.

"Remember to inform Major Plate and the general," said the private.

He handed the parchment to Lantern.

"This is for you, ma'am."

"A body," Lantern said, after the soldier had left. "We have never had much crime here. Now women are missing and there is a body."

"Crime comes with more people," said Genevieve. "We must not dwell on it. Look to our own lives. Don't give up hope concerning your Major Plate. You may have a future with him yet. We will ensnare him in our plans for Hayward Manchester. Compromise the both of them with us and then we have them."

"If the killer doesn't get one of us or both of us."

Genevieve narrowed her eyes perceptively. "I'm more afraid of Harkin getting here before we can accomplish our purposes than any killer."

Genevieve's demeanor was deceptive. She was now worried her mission, which she thought had been expertly accomplished, and her contact, whom she had found to be much different than her preconceived notions of a witch, were both in jeopardy.

She watched her cousin abstractedly as she pondered what to do next.

Lantern took the parchment the soldier had delivered and unsealed it.

"It is my notification. I have won a character!" she said excitedly.

Chapter 16

All over the colony, ticket holders for the masquerade ball were opening their character notifications. And they were reacting.

Except for the missing women, Thistle, Hortense, and Prudence.

"I was hoping for the Marquis de Lafayette," said Reverend Falldrem with disappointment. "Or General Washington."

"This silly party has just gotten even funnier," Mrs. Falldrem said. "You could not possibly look anything like the Czar of Russia."

"I agree. But we have to go by the rules. There's no switching."

"I'm glad I didn't get a specific character. I can make an ancient costume out of a simple bed sheet," said Mrs. Falldrem. "I'll be an ancient Roman..."

"I've been asked to arrive early and help prepare. So I will go on without you," Margaret Craig told her husband, the congressman, with disappointment.

"I will not see your costume before you get there?"

"I'm not making it myself. One of the privileges of being selected. I'll be measured for it tomorrow. And it must be a mistake that you did not draw a costume. I will check into it."

"This masquerade ball is a subterfuge," said Marchmont Craig. "You think we could reconsider and just stay home? I have to attend so many parties in Philadelphia these days. I get tired of parties."

"It is important to your future that we go. You won't have to spend all your time back east in the future."

"They are trying to displace me. I don't see how your being a part of this will make a difference."

"That's so wrong. You have done so much for the colony. They are just evil to want to turn you out."

Marchmont Craig put his hand on his wife's shoulder.

"Penberthy wants the senate. That should rightfully be mine. Worse they want to replace me with Manchester."

"That's what rubs the most. Manchester!"

"Yes. Only if Penberthy gets the presidency do I have a chance. I'm third choice."

"Penberthy? President? That's a joke. He's no longer even attractive like he used to be. He's gotten fat. A pot belly."

"More like soft flab, if you ask me."

"I'm soon going to have much more of a belly myself," she said, smiling.

He reached and rubbed her abdomen.

They let their delight at the prospect of a child overshadow their status worries for a moment.

In a short time the anxiety returned.

"We have to consider how we will live if I leave politics. It doesn't pay but all the peripheral opportunities to make a little money will be gone. I don't want to be a farmer."

"It won't happen. I won't let them do this to you. How can they?"

"They will just do it."

"What are they going to do?"

"Deny me the nomination. I will be relegated to the state house, if I even get that."

"I don't think so. There has to be a way to prevent this from happening."

"It's this damn ball. If only nobody important from the east shows up, it won't be so bad. Sort of like them putting on a concert with no one in the audience. But I'm told we're expecting Jefferson, Madison, or maybe even the President."

"No! Not coming here just to humiliate you?"

"A disaster, I agree. It is probably not true. Like the outrageous rumors that some of the monarchs of Europe will soon be arriving. Nonsense, but designed to get the petty bourgeois out in force. And snag maybe the governor or a minor central government figure. Hamilton perhaps."

"European kings! Lord help us."

"Well, pet, don't worry about it. Maybe it will all come to naught. There's one more thing though with all that's been going on and I hesitated to bring it up," said Marchmont.

"What?"

"The other day there was a meeting. Well, it was a masculine conference. But Reverend Falldrem did ask me to tell you something."

Haltingly Congressman Craig repeated the minister's request to his wife.

Tears came to Margaret's eyes.

"I have to leave the choir? After all these years? Who complained about my singing?"

"He didn't say. However, don't let it bother you. With the baby coming, you won't have time to waste being in a choir anyway..."

Father McKinsy looked at his notification letter in disbelief.

They've given me an impossible role to play. I'm going to complain. How could they expect me to portray Martin Luther?

It occurred to him that he did not know who would receive such a complaint. He had tried to discourage his few parishioners from joining such groups. As far as he knew, only the servant girl, Emilia, was in the organization.

No wait, he thought, recalling a bit of gossip. *There may be one of them at the convent...*

"Deborah Franklin!" Lantern complained to Genevieve.

"At least you got a character. I heard several prominent people were left out."

This did not cause Lantern to mince words.

"They expect me to portray Deborah Franklin? I didn't even know Mr. Franklin has a wife. I didn't even notice there was such a character listed. If he is married, how come we never hear anything about his wife?"

"She died in 1774," said Genevieve.

"You know about her?" Lantern called from the kitchen. She had stepped out to see if Emilia was beginning work on dinner yet.

"From somewhere in my pamphlet work. Maybe once when Ben-" she broke off.

"Once when you had been where?" Lantern asked, returning to the parlor.

"Maybe once I had been in a meeting one time where she was mentioned. A long time ago. I recall her described as a plain practical

69

person. Frugal and modest."

"I might have drawn Helen of Troy, Catherine the Great- but no- Deborah Franklin! It's so frustrating! Older women should get the plain characters!"

"Be thankful you don't have to make your own costume," Genevieve said.

Henri Mannstein opened Thistle's notification letter.

Helen of Troy.

How she would love to play such a part.

"Where are you Thistle? Please come back. I will forgive anything," he said softly.

"Don't you worry, Mr. Mannstein. That was the character she wanted and she'll be back to play it."

"No, Naomi. This selection was prepared before anyone knew of Thistle's disappearance. They will get someone else to be Helen."

"I think I should sew the costume for her and have it ready in case she comes back before that party happens," said Naomi.

"You can sew a costume that would fit her without her being here?"

"You just leave it to me," Naomi was saying. "I'll sew that costume and I'll get it ready and have it lying on the bed. When she gets back, it will be there for her. Let them give the part to somebody else. They'll just be two Helen of Troys at that party."

"Naomi," said Mannstein determinedly. "You go ahead and do that. After all, if she does come back and find out she was to be Helen of Troy and she has no gown, she will be heartbroken. And if you do make the costume and she does not come back?"

Mannstein broke off and swallowed hard.

"Don't think that way, Mr. Mannstein. She's going to be found. I feel in my heart she is alive."

Neilman Horaceton had much the same reaction to Prudence's notification. Only no one to talk about it with except his children who did not understand.

Hortense Melton's notification remained unopened.

Chapter 17

"The body was found by animals and a facial identification is not going to be possible. The body has been in the woods for some time. Animals got to the face, I believe."

"You need not go on. I will do my best to give a clear identification."

"I was just trying to prepare you, sir," said Major Plate.

They sat quietly waiting in the carriage until Mannstein was ready to get out and go in the convent.

He took a good look at Mannstein as he walked toward the corpse. Several solemn nuns watched them both.

The identification only took a moment.

"This is not Thistle," Mannstein said as he approached the dead woman. The relief in his voice was undeniable and that he broke down weeping was clearly a sign of joy, not disappointment.

"I'll have to bring in the other husband," Major Plate told the attending nuns quietly. "No one else is missing except for Hortense Melton. And her parents still insist she has gone back up the wilderness trail, on the way to visit friends east."

Plate told the sisters that Horaceton was on a journey for the supplies Prudence had never returned with. He would not be back immediately.

The body had to be buried, the nuns informed the soldier.

Identification by Horaceton would have to be made from clothing removed from the dead person.

"Preserve as much clothing as possible until he can get here," Major Plate pleaded. "We must know who this woman was."

The nuns agreed to prepare the body using the Weaving Mistress cloak, saving the garments the deceased had worn underneath.

"I need to hear again from you that you are sure," Major Plate said to Mannstein as they were traveling back to the Mannstein estate.

"Absolutely," Henri Mannstein declared. "Please continue to look for her."

"Certainly. I will do my best to keep trying to find her."

"I don't understand how anyone could not see that this is the work of those witches."

"Pardon?" Major Plate jerked the horse's reins a little guiltily as Mannstein's comment intruded on his thoughts about the hopelessness of finding Thistle Mannstein and the uncertainty of identification of a body by clothing only.

"I'm convinced those women have her. That group that is supposed to be in business, they are no more in business than the Indians are truly meaning to make peace. They are witches, a coven, a cult, they are up to no good in this land and I believe they have Thistle," said Henri Mannstein.

"But there's no evidence of that. Before he gave them permits to operate their business, General Leshoward thoroughly checked them out. They conduct their meetings outdoors in public. Anyone can attend and observe. I have done so. They do open their meetings with a rather simple prayer."

"I would almost bet that if you knew more about witches, you would find that that's not a prayer but an incantation."

"Nevertheless, they are following the law. Their activities are lawful. General Leshoward is determined there will be religious tolerance here in this colony and your own denomination has benefited."

"My own denomination is the true Christian faith! We are talking about paganism! And how do you know they don't have other meetings that you don't know anything about?"

"In a colony this small how could they keep it quiet? Your priest has not objected."

"He doesn't dare. He knows the Sisters of the Trinity Convent would come under attack if he did. Oh, these witches could keep it quiet if it was under the guise of a respectable operation. Like running this masquerade ball. Who knows what kind of trouble this is going to bring?"

"Yet you agreed to have the party in your home?" asked Major Plate.

"It is the first major affair for the colony since we all moved outside the fort and others began to relocate here. There was much social pressure to do that from the leaders of the colony and Thistle badly wanted it there."

"So if your wife has left of her own accord, you are thinking she will return for the festivities?" asked Major Plate. "You're just expecting her to return home? She will have no fear?"

"Thistle knows no fear. Especially of me. She knows how much I love her. This infernal gala, taking place at our home- Thistle had been so excited about it, so hopeful it would break some of the barriers for us," said Mannstein.

Major Plate could think of no reply.

As he took leave of the distressed husband, the similarity of the words coven and convent ran through the soldier's consciousness. He knew many in his own protestant denomination considered them synonyms.

Chapter 18

The general was still gone.

After a brief visit home the previous night, taking time to go by the convent and look at the clothing found in the woods, he was off again to the other side of the colony for another trivial dispute among the colonists.

He had informed the nuns that he did not recognize anything about the garments.

It was hard to tell.

He was sure it was not Abigail Fichton.

He left a message to that effect with Lantern to give to Major Plate.

Lantern found herself with a dilemma.

She was unchaperoned.

So brief a companion, Genevieve was now also gone.

Lantern had awoken to a note left by her cousin that she had to go into town unexpectedly.

Not to worry...

But she did not know when she would return.

Genevieve had left before dawn. She had taken her possessions.

Shortly after Emilia arrived and began working quietly in the kitchen, a violent rapping on the door startled them both.

"Stay in the kitchen, Emilia. It's nothing. I will get it."

She hid her concern from the maide but she put her pistol in her skirt pocket and cautiously approached the front door.

She cracked it open.

The figure was clearly delineated in the morning sunlight as he stood tapping his boots impatiently.

"Major Plate!" She rushed to fling the door open wide. The major rarely visited the general's house during working hours although it was just a 15 minute walk across the courtyard.

The time he had spent with Lantern had always been in the early evening under the general's watchful eye and an occasional meeting in town at the tea shop during lunch hour on Saturdays.

He had never come to the general's home before when he knew

the general was gone. And never to the front door!

He explained how he did have permission from her father and since his office was officially in the house, it could be put down to his waiting to see the general.

Plus, her cousin's presence would mediate.

Lantern awkwardly explained Genevieve was absent.

After a short reflection they decided to ignore that circumstance.

Both trusted the other not to force a betrothal on a technicality.

"I wanted to check in on you and make sure you are okay. Two, possibly three or four women in the colony have disappeared and there has been a body found. We are trying to identify it from clothing," said Major Plate.

"I know about the body. My father says to tell you it is not Abigail Fichton or anyone he knows as far as he could tell. Who is missing and who has died?" Lantern asked.

"Then the dead woman is still not identified. Yet. And I admit a surreptitious reason for my visit. I would like your insight on the subject of the missing women."

"I will do anything I can to help."

"You are up to date on contemporary society and politics. I want your opinion about a society woman named Thistle Mannstein. Surely, you know of her. And a schoolmaster's wife, Prudence Horaceton. That's the first thing."

He took a deep breath.

Lantern looked at him expectantly, assuming he understood she knew none of the people by sight.

"Then I have to tell you about a woman named Ruthanne Webber. That is, unless your father has mentioned her?" asked Major Plate.

"He hasn't mentioned anyone by that name."

Major Plate gave her a concise summary of all he knew about the missing women and the dead body.

As superior to all the other soldiers and subordinate to the general, Major Plate had few people he could converse with on an equal level in the area.

Lantern was his primary friend.

He told her everything he knew.

"You think Mr. Mannstein murdered his wife out of jealousy. Mr. Horaceton did away with his wife because she didn't get along with his children. Because Hortense Melton is single, you think she ran off with some serious suitor or was the victim of someone who likes to kill young women. And you think that the deceased is none of these three women," said Lantern, summarizing.

She was joking a little, was trying to hide her disappointment that Major Plate was remaining so formal and suppress the small thrill she felt with him being so near with no chaperon.

Major Plate smiled.

He enjoyed Lantern's sense of humor.

"Ruthanne Webber saw the deceased before burial and declared the body is not Hortense. Her parents are not available to make an identification. They had set out for Philadelphia to try to find her. This leaves Mrs. Horaceton. Neilman Horaceton is off on a supply trip but I expect he will recognize his wife's garments."

"Your instincts are probably right," she said seriously.

"As far as the Mannstein woman, it is not a case of murder yet. Not even death. There's no evidence to indicate that Thistle Mannstein is not alive. There's no evidence at all. Period. She has just disappeared. Same with Hortense Melton."

"I will have to think about it. Why don't you let me have the day servant make us tea? Emilia!"

While Lantern gave instructions to Emilia and they waited for tea, the conversation continued.

"There does not seem much mystery to me about the schoolmaster's wife."

"Prudence Horaceton?"

"I would think she left her husband because she did not want to care for his children. It was too much for her. She had taken on more than she bargained for and there would never be any money. His wanting her to start working at a job outside the home was probably the final straw. That is anathema to most women."

Major Plate had not considered that possibility.

"And what about Ruthanne Webber? Is she missing also?"

76

Lantern asked, a little facetiously.

Major Plate hesitated.

Lantern was important to him. Her feelings mattered.

He treasured her friendship.

General Leshoward was his commanding officer, as dear to him as his own father.

In the society in which they lived, the general's official authority was also accompanied by moral authority over the lives of his men.

"Yes. About Ruthanne Webber, I need to tell you something," he said.

He took a deep breath.

"I have been instructed by your father..."

Chapter 19

There was time for no more conversation as a messenger knocked on the door and Emilia came out of the kitchen.

It was a good time to stop.

Lantern had lost track of her emotions.

"It's a messenger from the Penberthy's home," said Emilia, upon answering the door. The messenger left quickly and she repeated his words. "Major Plate is to come over there at once."

Plate said goodbye quickly and left.

Emilia returned to the kitchen.

Lantern stood near the front door and the sudden shock of what he had just told her hit.

He was as good as betrothed to Ruthanne Webber.

Tears came and she had an urge to run.

Run somewhere, just run away. She could no longer stand her surroundings.

She stumbled towards the kitchen, intending to run past Emilia as she made her way to the back door.

But the kitchen was empty and the back door was open.

Lantern brushed the tears from her cheeks and slowed down. A little curiosity blossomed.

Emilia was just outside the back door talking to someone in the cold.

A man.

And he didn't sound like one of the soldiers.

Lantern listened for a few moments before her brain deciphered the accent on the words she was hearing.

"She has gone to the printer shop. I don't think she was coming back," the man was saying.

Lantern flung the door open.

Emilia gasped and jumped. The man beside her remained calm.

"Who are you?" Lantern demanded.

The man stepped away from Emilia, clicked his boots and scowled as he bowed.

"I am Fabric, Mistress. I am trespassing. The soldiers from

across the courtyard should be called."

"No!" Emilia said.

"Miss Emilia is not to blame for my presence."

"Yes I am!" Emilia said. "I invited him. We were in the kitchen while you were visiting with Major Plate."

"It's cold out here. Let's go inside," said Lantern.

She held the door so that the slave and servant girl had to go in before her. Then she led them all the way to the parlor.

"Now," she said, shutting the kitchen door behind her. "Who were you talking about going to the print shop?"

Emilia and Fabric looked at each other.

"He was speaking of Mistress Genevieve. He was just repeating what I told him."

"You know what happened with Mistress Genevieve?"

"She told me she was just on a short errand," said Emilia.

"And take all of her possessions? She left a note saying that she was going to town," Lantern said.

"Maybe she was going to stop at the print shop on her way out of town," suggested Fabric.

"Fabric, hush. Mistress, Fabric is my- I mean that he and I-"

"I am not oblivious as to what goes on," said Lantern.

"The general knows about our friendship," said Fabric.

"He certainly did not tell me," Lantern said.

"The general was hoping that Fabric might move to the fort and help out some," Emilia said hesitantly.

Lantern paused. "We could certainly use help. In what capacity would you come?"

"That's the problem," said Fabric. "I don't have a legal status."

"I see. I think since my father isn't here you need to just go back to where you came from for the time being."

"Yes, Mistress, I will," said Fabric.

"Mistress Lantern, may I get him a few things from the kitchen? He brought us some potatoes and I thought I would return some squash," said Emilia.

"Of course," said Lantern. "Potatoes were scarce recently. I thank you."

Emilia turned and went to the kitchen, leaving Lantern and Fabric alone in the parlor.

"And why are you called Fabric?" Lantern asked, trying to hide her nervousness.

"I do not know, Mistress. It is just what I have always been called."

"How do you spell it? Like a piece of cloth?" Lantern asked.

"I don't know how to spell it. I cannot read or write. I am a slave. It is illegal for me to be able to read or write."

"Oh yes, of course. But you speak such perfect English."

"My mother was a slave in England. She was sold to a planter immigrating to the colonies and, as she carried me at the time, I had no choice but to come with her. The planter was kind enough to allow her to raise me to the age of 14 before he sold me to the family that brought me to Kentucky."

"And what of that family?" Lantern asked.

"They all perished in the last influenza, Mistress. They had no living relatives to inherit me."

"I hear you live alone out here in the woods?"

"Yes, quite nicely. Until someone comes to claim me or kill me or chain me."

"I'm certainly not going to do that. I'm General Leshoward's daughter and I can promise you protection of the fort if you come to be with us," Lantern said.

"I will give it a great deal of thought."

"When my father gets back we will try to work out a solution."

"Mistress Lantern, why are you named so strangely?"

Lantern told him with no hesitation. She had repeated the story so many times it came naturally to her whenever the question was asked.

"I am told it was because when I was born my mother bade me be a light to the world. At least that's what she told my father. I have no memories of her. She died during the revolution."

Emilia returned.

"Here is the squash," she said.

Lantern took a deep breath. She was not a judgmental person but she had responsibilities that went with her status.

"Emilia, you seem to be more than just acquainted with Fabric?"

"Yes, Mistress," said Emilia.

"You meet with him often?" Lantern asked.

"At least once a week, Mistress," said Emilia.

"I see," Lantern said.

There is somebody for everyone except me, thought Lantern. *Even the kitchenmaide.*

"Just remember propriety. We can have no scandal at the fort."

What am I saying? thought Lantern. *I can't even let them know I have these type of thoughts. Yet I have to. It's my responsibility. Heavens! What am I going to say when they ask me what I'm talking about?*

Fabric and Emily seemed to understand perfectly.

"I need to ask. When you meet, where do you go, and what do you do?"

"We meet in different places. Sometimes in the cabin I share with the soldiers' cook when she is not there, in good weather, or if I could get a ride out on the grounds of the cabin near where he camps, sometimes here when you and the general are away. Please do not punish him," said Emilia.

"I'm not going to punish anyone. I'm just trying to make sure that nothing has happened that would bring scandal to the fort."

"I may be but a kitchen maiden but I'm true to my creed."

"Your creed?"

Don't tell me she's a witch, too? Lantern thought silently.

"The Apostles Creed. I am teaching it to Fabric. You asked what we do. That's what we do. At least part of the time," said Emilia.

They looked at each other and smiled.

Lantern felt a cold chill. That could be interpreted as teaching him to read. She tried to recall if that was actually illegal in this part of the United States. She wasn't sure.

Teaching him in the name of religion however was probably allowed under this new constitution.

"Just keep quiet about it," Lantern said.

"We are most discreet, Mistress."

"You're Catholic, Emilia?" Lantern asked.

"Yes, Mistress," said Emilia.

"How about that? I didn't even know. Are you religious, Fabric?"

"I don't know, Mistress." He looked down at her as Emilia looked up at him hopefully. "It may turn out that way."

Chapter 20

Called from Lantern's side just after informing her about Ruthanne, all thoughts of both women vanished from Major Plate's mind as he looked at Jane Penberthy.

She had summoned someone in authority.

They stood on her front lawn before the remains of a dismembered animal.

"I would hardly think the murder of a sheep would've called for the second-in-command from the fort to come out here," said Jane.

"You asked for a high ranking official. The general is occupied with plans for the gala."

Major Plate was surprised by how the sweetness in Jane's voice brought back memories of their aborted courtship as she continued to talk.

"I jest. I am discovering it just now. I didn't see it before I came out to greet you. I sent a messenger to the fort about a different matter. I want to speak to someone about Thistle Mannstein."

"Do you know her well?" asked Major Plate.

"She's a friend. Now that I'm Lutheran, we have something in common. We were both at the mercy of the tolerance in the colony for other religions. I have more in common with Thistle than I do the women of my congregation. Can you understand that?"

"Easily."

Jane and Thistle Mannstein were very wealthy women. That would supersede denomination for many people.

"Rumors are these disappearances have happened before and are somehow connected to other men," said Major Plate frankly.

He did not tell Jane about the body of the unknown woman who was not Thistle. He did not speak of a connection between the missing women and the animal on her lawn.

Major Plate saw no need to alarm her.

Maybe there was no connection. The dead animal, reminiscent of a religious sacrifice, might be misguided anti-Lutheranism.

A gesture more likely to be aimed at a Catholic household, provided the bigot was educated.

It had been Major Plate's experience that most vandals were not educated.

The two people turned and walked away from the carcass. Jane Partington Penberthy had plenty of servants to take care of the mess.

"No. I know she has gone away in the past. But not without her husband at least thinking that he knows where she is. And I don't believe it has anything to do with any other man."

Major Plate took Jane Penberthy's hand. "You have my word. I am taking Thistle Mannstein's disappearance seriously."

"Thank you," Jane said.

Reginald Penberthy joined his wife after Major Plate left.

"Why didn't you come out and say hello?" she asked.

"I don't take these things slightly. You were one step away from being betrothed to the man when I stepped up and let my feelings be known."

Jane bit her lip.

"It wasn't meant to be. I would never have come to the correct church but through you."

"It's still awkward to have him in the community."

Jane rubbed her head, which began to ache.

Chapter 21

The Melton farm, where Ruthanne Webber now resided, featured a modest farmhouse with several thoroughbred horses stabled there among many more common equines.

A clairvoyant had predicted Kentucky would someday be known for horse farms.

That day had not yet come.

Major Plate had little interest in horses. He was going to visit Ruthanne. He had been invited before the Meltons had abruptly left for Philadelphia.

Ruthanne had assured him the invitation stood.

"I don't take with the old rules concerning chaperons anyway. We fought a war to have more freedom and create a society where men and women can behave as responsible adults without supervision," she said.

Shown to a sitting area by a houseslave, they would be dining alone.

"I have no family to look after my interests and I am relying on your reputation as a gentleman and a man of his word to avoid scandal."

Her fresh and glowing beauty erased all political thoughts from his mind, almost all thoughts of Thistle Mannstein, Prudence Horaceton, and their disappearances.

He even had no thoughts of Hortense Melton.

Although he was in her home.

Ruthanne's presence was overwhelming and she had made the place her own.

The slave came in to announce the dinner was ready. Ruthanne took Plate's arm and they went into the dining room.

"I hope you do forgive me for not letting on about my purpose for coming to Kentucky when I first came to your office," said Ruthanne. "I was afraid it might embarrass you that I knew about our proposed courtship before you did."

"Truthfully, it is a little embarrassing."

"I hope you don't think this is my idea. The general has kept in touch with me all these years but until the last of my family died his letters were only a formality."

"I do know that he has taken a personal interest in widows of the men lost under his command. All but a few have remarried or otherwise seen their widowhoods come to a close."

"When I wrote to him that I would be coming to live with the Meltons, he wrote me back about you and portrayed you in a very favorable light. I had assumed he had also done the reverse when speaking to you. Although I realize he doesn't really know me in the way that he knows you."

"The general has been like a father to me. Serving under him has been the only life I have known since I was a boy. I came from a large family and had to seek my fortune. When he took me on as his personal aide, I felt like I had found a job for life."

"It sounds like your agreement to court me is tantamount to following orders. So we are here alone with servants and slaves, this will seal our marriage or compromise me. Surely, you know that."

Major Plate was silent.

"No matter. I am firmly of the belief that love comes between a man and a woman over time. It was that way with my first husband and it shall be that way with you. I hope you do find me pleasant?"

"Indeed, you could not be more pleasant."

"I hope it's not a problem that I tend to dress in a color that some people find bold?"

"I like red."

"Good. I use it for most of my winter garments. An extravagance. For summer I go to pink."

"Believe me the colors of your clothing are not anything that I would give a whole lot of thought to," said Major Plate.

"I feel like I live in a world in which most women are all the same and this is my way of distinguishing myself just a little bit."

The slaves began to serve and Major Plate had a few moments to contemplate Ruthanne's remark about the similarity of women.

It struck him for the first time how few women he had known in his life beyond his mother and sisters. Of those he was acquainted with, the only similarities he saw were limited to their clothing, especially if they were members of the Weaving Mistress group.

Between the woman he had courted unsuccessfully, Jane, and the woman he had contemplated courting, Lantern, he saw absolutely no similarity.

And in the woman he was assigned to court, daintily eating her food in small bites, he saw no similarity to the other two.

Ruthanne ate barely a tenth of her meal before she declared herself finished.

Major Plate began eating more hurriedly for he saw that he was going to have to abandon his food to keep her company.

He was still hungry when they left the table to walk out and sit in the porch swing.

The slaves discreetly accompanied them outside and found positions under trees, sitting on the ground in such a way that it was not apparent that they could still see or hear the white couple.

Major Plate knew that any discrepancy in his behavior would be reported, if not to the absent Meltons, to General Leshoward.

Ruthanne was very calm and demure as she chatted about the potential life they would have together.

Before the evening was over, she had their entire life for the next 10 years arranged.

All Major Plate was going to need to do was appear at the proper time and place to fulfill his role in her scenario.

When he waved goodbye to her, it occurred to him that she was singularly unaware that there was only social convention to stop him from fulfilling the role.

His term in the army was up before the June statehood convention.

While his social position in Leverageton would be decimated after having spent this evening with her without proper chaperons, he could travel to any other part of the United States, stake his claim there, and start over.

Ruthanne, on the other hand, would be ruined socially for life. Her very words indicated she had known that without a doubt when she had told him to keep his date with her despite the Meltons having left for Philadelphia.

Either she was very naive.
Very sure of her charm with him.
Or she didn't care.
Major Plate did not think Ruthanne was naive.
She was indeed charming.
She did seem to care.
He puzzled over his bride-to-be all the way home.

Chapter 22

Genevieve was her uncle's guest, a situation that could not last.

She had taken steps to remedy it and was again in the printer's shop.

This time to stay.

She put her personal belongings upstairs but immediately came down to work.

By the dim light of the oil lamp, Genevieve looked at the other papers that she had also prepared.

She knew she could trust the printer to execute them without asking any questions.

In the daytime, he functioned as printer for the colony for the newspaper, pamphlets, and private needs of the socially minded.

At night, his shop was available for more serious pursuits.

Anything needing a discreet printing could be inserted into a large folder with payment and a notation of when it would be picked up or where it should be sent.

That was the weak point in the chain.

And Genevieve's desire to help a servant had overcome her natural precautionary nature.

She did not know the people she was helping very well.

Had barely met them.

Her contact had explained their dilemma, knowing Genevieve had the skills to help.

It was a matter of principle and belief for Genevieve.

A life changing action for those involved.

It was a risk and if it went wrong, Genevieve would be more than lost to that cause. She could face prison, under certain circumstances even execution.

She looked at the papers.

There was a fire crackling in the fireplace.

She could easily toss the parchment into the flames and it would rapidly burn, the threads woven within it melting in the heat, the wood slivers turning to ashes.

She walked over to the fireplace and held up the paper.

She looked at the fire once more, then took the paper and rolled it and hid it within her cloak.

Turning her back on the hearth, she prepared to exit the print shop to make her way to her next destination.

The shop door burst open and a figure holding a gun stood before her.

Chapter 23

"I want to know what's going on! Why are you here? What are you doing? Have you betrayed us to the British?"

"Lantern! The war is long over. Put the gun down."

"No! We know there are plots. Since you arrived at this colony look at what all has happened!"

"I can explain-"

"My father is taking mysterious trips without me. My male suitor has abandoned me for your traveling companion," Lantern said.

"She was not actually my companion."

"Two women have disappeared, possibly three, with one murdered."

"I know nothing about that."

"Evidence of animal sacrifice has been found in the colony," Lantern said.

"Or that."

"My kitchenmaide appears and disappears like the sun on a partial cloud day," Lantern said.

Genevieve was silent.

"I want to know what is going on."

Getting over her astonishment that her young cousin had such audacity as to defy the curfew and initiative to track her to the print shop, Genevieve began putting together a cover story.

"Lantern. Put the gun down. I am not your enemy. Listen to what I say."

"You will tell me all you know about what is going on or I will take actions that will lead to others making you talk. You think I am just your young cousin. The general's spoiled daughter. But I can assure you there is more to me though I only be 17 years, my mind is as fully competent and functioning as yours."

"I don't doubt that at all, Lantern. If you will just put the gun down I will tell you. Please, why not trust me?" Genevieve asked.

Lantern slowly dropped the pistol down on a table. She sat near the table while her cousin made herself comfortable closer to the fire.

"Here, take a look at this paper that I have prepared."

"What has this to do with the Weaving Mistresses and witchcraft and the missing and murdered women?" Lantern asked.

"Nothing. These are for Fabric and Emilia. They are going away together."

Lantern took a moment to reconsider.

"Why didn't you tell me you were trying to help Fabric and Emilia?"

"I didn't know you knew anything about their love affair."

"I didn't until just the other day. I sort of caught them in the kitchen," Lantern said.

"One reason I didn't tell you is because what I'm doing is illegal and could get us all in jail and my uncle dismissed from the army if scandal reached up to him."

"He is a great general. He won a great victory."

"That was years ago. People forget. He would be disgraced. You'd lose your enviable position here at Fort Leverage."

"You can trust me not reveal anything," Lantern said.

"Yes, I think I can trust you. In fact, I'm going to trust you with the papers."

Genevieve hesitated. She then took a small knife and ripped the pocket where the envelope was sewn in. She rose and went over to the table. When she turned back around she gave Lantern a sealed envelope.

"Keep that safe with you until we need it. Emilia is not completely sure that she wants to go with Fabric. He's waiting for her to make up her mind. Once she does, either way he will need these papers. Can I trust you to keep them safe?" Genevieve asked.

"Oh absolutely!"

"You must not open or tamper with these. It will negate their effectiveness. Emilia and Fabric will suffer," said Genevieve.

"You can trust me to take care of them."

"And not open them."

"Of course," Lantern said.

"If you do open and read them, they are worthless and you must destroy them," Genevieve emphasized.

"I want for Emilia and Fabric to be together. Even if it means losing our only servant. She doesn't do that much anyway anymore. It seems she's thinking of him all day long," Lantern said.

"All right. I'm trusting you with their lives."

"Why don't you come back to fort? Surely now the estrangement in our family is over."

"Not if your father is going to try to marry me to Harkin. In fact, I'm not leaving town after all. I'm staying here above the print shop just like I normally do when I'm at work. I've worked it out with the printer. He has an overwhelming amount of work with all these new people coming in and no competitor yet."

"I can't say that I blame you. Father's matchmaking," said Lantern, shaking her head. "He has betrothed Major Plate to Ruthanne Webber."

"Yes I know. She told me about that on the way from Philadelphia. I didn't want to mention it to you. You were so sure about him just a few days ago. I know it will be difficult for you."

"So you know my daydreams were fantasies. Well, I don't want to talk about it. There's nothing to do. I wish you would reconsider not coming back," Lantern said.

"No."

"By the way." Lantern's tone changed slightly. "What is Ruthanne like? Will she make Major Plate happy, do you think? I hope nothing has been said about my friendship with him."

"She never mentioned you and neither did I. She seemed to think Major Plate was previously courting Jane Partington before she married Penberthy. That must be what my uncle told her. I don't know her. She was a nice companion for the long journey. Speaking of which, you need to get back to the fort. I can ride back with you."

"That's not necessary. I have a robe. I will put it on so I won't be stopped. I will be fine," Lantern said.

"That's good because I've got work to do," said Genevieve under her breath as Lantern left the print shop.

Genevieve put her robe on and also her veil. Her work was not in the shop this time.

Chapter 24

Lantern started slowly riding back towards the fort but stopped as soon as she could safely hide and watch the printer's shop. As she anticipated, Genevieve departed soon after, going into the woods.

Lantern followed.

The night was clear.

It became easy to track her cousin when she veered off into the woods, for having no idea she was being followed, Genevieve made noise.

Genevieve reached the abandoned cabin, tied up her horse, and went inside.

Lantern could see in the window. The room was designed like a church. Rows of benches without backs were placed to accommodate listeners.

All exterior features of every woman were completely covered except their eyes. Lantern counted 15 near identical figures settled in the chairs arranged before a small podium.

The woman who came to address them from that podium wore identical clothing, also complete with veil and gloves.

Lantern had not seen the veils until recently. She knew she could not slip into the group without one.

Voices raised from within.

She froze, clearly hearing the words.

"Mistresses, you know why you are here. You are the believers."

Another exterior voice behind her hissed as the interior ones dissolved into approving chatter.

"Lantern! What on earth are you doing here?"

Lantern turned slightly and found herself closer to Major Plate than she had ever been.

He was clutching her waist and pulling her towards him.

Her heart pounded.

"I saw one of them in the street and I followed her. What are you doing here?" she asked calmly.

"I seem to be the only one interested in solving the murder. Nobody else cares about anything except politics, this masquerade ball, and witches!" Major Plate complained to Lantern as if their meeting in the woods and eavesdropping on secret meetings were a commonplace occurrence.

"What did you know about this?"

"It was suggested to me these women met in secret. Fabric camps in alternating spots near here and he has observed them meeting here, not often, only on fair nights. I believe this is some sort of religious service held by that small segment which is always veiled. How did you come to be here? Don't tell me you are one of them, trying to get into the ceremony?"

"No, I just have a robe for traveling after curfew. Father is away so much at nights these days. I fear having to go after him someday. Tonight I went after Genevieve." Lantern hoped he would accept her explanation about the robe as easily as Genevieve did.

"I know most of the women in town have sewn a robe so they can travel at will at night. But how did you get here?"

"I followed one of them," Lantern told him again.

"Listen, Leverageton is no longer the safe place it used to be. A few years ago it was safe for women to travel alone and for the youth of the colony to gather for games and fun, night or day. But that was a brief moment in time. Our colony has started attracting attention with our tolerant and peaceful way of life and less peaceful people are moving here. Why do you think your father has to make so many trips outside of the fort now that there is a courthouse?"

"He said the building of a courthouse caused it to be used."

"Nonsense. There are more disputes, trials, and troubled conflicts, because there are more people. Bad now intermingles with the good. Established relationships are displaced. We became complacent in just a short time with a safe and easy existence. Look how quickly that changed. Would you have believed just a short time ago that women could disappear from our community?"

"Do you think the women that have disappeared are related to this group?" Lantern asked.

Both people realized the chatter within the walls of the cabin had ceased and a clear voice was speaking again.

"Do you think the women are here tonight?" Lantern whispered excitedly. "Look, some of them have their children in there. The little girls have witch's hats and flags!"

"It just looks like children playing to me. Sh, yes, maybe. Listen to what they have to say," said Major Plate.

It was too late. The voices had deteriorated back to chatter. There was acquiescent murmuring amongst the women.

Chants began in another language neither Plate nor Lantern understood.

The eavesdropping couple stepped away.

"Perhaps you are overreacting to the idea that this group of women feels like they need to meet in secret in order to accomplish their goals without harassment. Did you not take my opinions into account from when we talked the other day?"

"Yes, and God preserve us. I hope you are right. I hope Prudence Horaceton just left. But I do think that Thistle Mannstein has been temporarily abducted. My best guess is someone does not want her to be Helen of Troy at this masquerade ball."

"How can that be connected to this group?" Lantern asked.

"Lantern, use your common sense. They are organizing the event."

"Have you ever caught them meeting like this before?"

"Yes, but it was raining and I could not hear anything. And they're not doing anything illegal," said the soldier.

"They have right of assembly under the new constitution."

"But I don't like it. I need to get you back to the fort before we are found here together. Take off that infernal robe. I know why you wear it but I think you would be better off with the nun's clothing. Why don't you get a copy of a nun's habit? It will afford the same nighttime travel privilege."

"I don't know. Because they might take me to their convent and keep me there if they catch me. I am afraid of nuns," Lantern said.

"Nonsense. Nuns won't hurt you."

He grasped her shoulders and she found her hands pressed against his chest.

She put her cheek to his and closed her eyes.

He took a deep breath and gripped her tighter.

A sound from within the cabin distracted them. Musical chants arose louder in the wilderness.

He relaxed his hold on her.

Lantern turned away.

As he brought the horses from the bushes, she gazed back to the window at the group of women.

A few had now removed their veils. The meeting was coming to an end.

She stiffened. In the dim lamplight, she thought she saw not one but two familiar faces that she could not place.

And one that she could- Emilia.

Genevieve and Emilia!

Both involved!

Major Plate was coming back towards her.

Lantern turned, blocking him from the view of the window, hoping he would not see Emilia. They mounted quietly.

As they rode away, they heard scattered applause.

Chapter 25

Lantern and Major Plate had been wrong. The secret meeting of the Weaving Mistresses was not ending. It was just beginning.

Most left. However, as sunrise approached, there were a few women left at the gathering.

They retained their veils.

Before the dawn could break, a newcomer arrived.

She was welcomed personally by the Mistress Superior...

"Our newest recruit has arrived," the Mistress spoke up.

The other women grew quiet.

Benches were moved so the newcomer could lie face first flat on the floor.

She was helped into a prone position.

"Mistress, most high, I prostrate myself before thee."

The leader regarded the woman at her feet and suppressed a laugh.

The newcomer was helped up in silence and all stood as the Mistress Superior took a box and stood near the fireplace.

From the box she held up a cross, a talisman with a pentagram, and tarot cards. And threated to toss them all in the fire.

"Superstitious nonsense," she said aloud. "You agree?"

She placed the symbols on the edge of the hearth, in danger of the flames.

The newcomer lurched forward. Others grabbed her arms and held her back.

"Which symbol would you save if they let you go? I wonder. Never mind. Let her loose."

The Mistress Superior retrieved all of the symbols and put them back in the box.

"We see your distress. We, the small few in this room and a few others unable to be here, are the core of this group. We care nothing for selling cloth. We aspire to change the world. To bring down those who rule over us. You aspire to be one of us? Why?"

"I'm dissatisfied with religion. I want to learn the dark arts."

"But religion is not our purpose here. Any kind. Our ceremonies

98

are universal. We accept all forms of belief. Some even claim to be Christians."

The newcomer tried again. "There must be more to this world."

"There is much more. And once you learn them, what you do with the dark arts is entirely your affair. Our purpose differs."

"I- I want to better myself as a woman."

"You were in the right place, then. Forgive me if I don't immediately trust you, though you were sponsored by someone high up. We normally keep newcomers in the dark for a long time doing frivolous work such as sewing costumes. However, your sponsor was adamant that your initiation was urgent."

The Mistress Superior addressed the others for advice.

"Shall I remove my veil?"

Nods came all around. Approval of the newcomer was unanimous.

"In private then. The rest of you go. I will risk only myself."

Admiration for the courage of their leader ran high as the others left, still safely hidden behind their own veils.

Alone with the newest recruit, the Mistress removed her headpiece.

The newcomer gasped and had to sit down.

"I cannot believe it- YOU!"

"Your identity is as much a surprise to me as mine is to you. I knew you aspired to the social status of charitable works to benefit a poor widow. But I had no idea you were so committed."

"How is your voice so different?"

"I have perfected an accent to pass here in America. But in my group I do not use it. I can speak as myself. I delight in that small compensation." She paused. "You are valuable to us. What is it you really want from us?"

"I aspire to the black robe."

The new recruit began to undress.

The leader stopped her.

"Don't be silly, it's just an expression. If there were actually such a garment you would have to make it yourself, dye it yourself, and keep it hidden. Let no one ever know that you had it. It's merely a symbol. We wear robes of ordinary blue cloth."

"I see. I'm sorry. I'm very new to this."

"Which gets me back to your motives."

"I'm dissatisfied. Lonely. My talents are wasted in this society where I exist only as an object."

"I understand. Perfect. My own feelings are much the same. Very well. I have a small errand for you to get you started. It is a test. But easy. Something for you to deliver to Prudence Horaceton's husband. A note that will comfort and perhaps even relieve some of his distress," said the headmistress, still whispering.

"The schoolmaster's wife. One of you- us?"

"Surprisingly yes. You know where they live?"

"I do. I can deliver a message."

"Be cautious. Stay behind the veil. Do not reveal your identity to him."

"I will do it in the morning."

"Wonderful. Now let's talk about you. I feel I hardly know you. Tell me about yourself, about your life, about those you love, and about those you hate..."

Chapter 26

"Major Plate has expressed some concerns to me about the Weaving Mistress enterprise," said Marchmont Craig.

"Who is Major Plate?" Margaret asked.

"Leshoward's second-in-command at the fort."

"Oh yes. Him."

"He is considering starting an inquiry into the group's activities."

"Absolutely not. You must prevent that. Who does he think he is? We have been wary that authorities are becoming concerned about our success and trying to think up ways to stop us."

"I don't think that would be constitutional under the new document," said Marchmont thoughtfully.

"We're doing nothing illegal. Surely as a congressman you can to something to stop any inquiry?"

"I'm not sure that is lawful either."

"No one outside of our group needs to know anything about activities in the movement."

"Why is your group so secretive? It seems to be less like a business and more like a club."

"We have a right to keep our activities private to our members."

"What does go on? The military is not the only ones starting to suspect the Mistresses are doing more than just weaving and selling cloth."

Margaret sighed happily and gave her husband a sly look.

"It's far more exciting than I had hoped for," she said.

Marchmont Craig rose to the bait. "Tell me, just a little. I am your husband. I will keep it in confidence and knowing a little might help me fend them off."

"We think women will be a political force in the future," said Margaret Craig. "Already women have the vote in New Jersey. We want to establish a framework for the day when it comes to Kentucky. When women can vote."

"Brash actions can cause the loss of such privileges. Voting? Is that what it is all about?"

"What else could it be? And we have to obtain the privilege

before we can lose it."

"Okay." Marchmont Craig turned to leave.

"Wait a minute! I haven't told you who- we do have support in high places. This gala is an opportunity to solicit support by proving what an asset we can be to any organization."

"Whose support are you trying to get?"

"We hear Thomas Jefferson is coming."

"Don't count on that."

"We are told Jefferson is coming and coming for a purpose. To meet and pass political judgment on leaders here in Leverageton. This is going to be an opportunity for you, Marchmont."

"It is going to be an opportunity for Hayward Manchester and Reginald Penberthy."

"What are you saying?"

"If Jefferson comes, it will be to pick one of them to be a national leader."

"That must explain the costume selections list."

"I thought they were going to draw for costumes."

"No, that was just a subterfuge. They matched the right people to the right costumes. And I thought there was a mistake about you."

"No costume for me?"

"No! And my appeal was denied. My costume has been completed though. You can just wear formal attire if you like."

"Yes, we are short on money. I've none for a silly costume. A political group. Women voting! Well, that explains a lot. I will give Plate and Leshoward some double talk. It's a relief in a way. Much better than them being witches."

"Witches? Wherever did you hear that?"

"They're not really witches are they?"

"Don't be silly, of course not."

As he left she picked up her costume and slipped it on.

"Oh, darn," she said aloud to herself. "What will I do? I don't have time to alter this dress."

She was unable to fasten the gown. It was way too little in the waist.

And these old world gowns look just like slips, she thought, as she fingered it, trying to see a way to fix it.

That was an idea.

She was going to be wearing the Weaving Mistress robe over the top of it anyway. She would just not take off the robe and her own slip would appear enough alike so no one would notice.

As she stashed the too-small garment in her bureau, she pictured her new friend who had delivered the costume earlier, along with her instructions.

An important friend who had made it clear every rule must be obeyed.

She was a little uneasy at defying one of the rules so soon. But what could she do?

Nature was taking its course and she was liable to be even bigger by the day of the ball.

She patted her belly. She had not thought she would swell so much so soon.

Her heart pounded with excitement.

Chapter 27

"I am a friend of Prudence. A Weaving Mistress."

Neilman Horaceton remained on his horse. He had just returned home.

A robed and veiled woman carried a basket of cloth from which she pulled a sealed envelope and pointed it towards him.

"I've come to lend support. I know you are about to contact the soldier about the body they found."

"I was going to change clothes before letting the major know that I was back," Horaceton mumbled as he dismounted. He was uncomfortable talking to people without fully seeing their faces.

"I'm just here to deliver this message of sympathy and implore you to read it. And also implore you to attend the gala as had been planned. Prudence would want- would have wanted you to be there."

"Thank you," said Horaceton, taking the envelope.

"Promise me you will read this message before going to see the soldier. Before viewing the unfortunate woman's effects. It will give you much needed comfort and strength for the ordeal to come."

Behind the holes in the facial covering, the woman's eyes glittered as she held him back from opening his front door.

"I promise. My absolute word."

I didn't realize those Weaving Mistress women were some kind of religious group but that one had a pure fanatical look about her eyes, was his first analysis of her behavior.

Then he had second idea. Maybe it was not fanaticism.

There were no strong drugs, opiates, or drink allowed in the colony. Maybe this group had somehow obtained them or was making them.

Maybe that was what they were selling in addition to cloth.

He considered, then rejected the idea of advancing this possibility to authorities.

No one ever listened to him anyway.

He opened the letter and began reading.

Chapter 28

"There have been signs of animal sacrifice found on the Penberthy lawn?" asked Leshoward.

"Early this morning Horaceton identified the deceased's clothing as belonging his wife, Prudence," Major Plate reported.

"Could it be someone is preying on the Weaving Mistresses?" asked Leshoward.

"Prudence Horaceton was not part of that group. Or so her husband said. Yet the deceased was wearing a cloak over regular clothing when found."

"If Horaceton is sure that was his wife, that's where we will let the matter stand. She must have been secretly part of them. Wearing the veil like so many. Perhaps she had actually left him and found sanctuary with them. Then he found her."

"I have also found out that Thistle Mannstein has been known to go off before. She has been known to take trips to Philadelphia and New York. This in addition to the rumors that there have been other men involved."

"You will see to it none of this interferes with the gala tomorrow. I wish it were being held elsewhere."

"There may be a connection. Romantic trouble was originally thought to be behind the disappearance of the third girl, the Melton girl, the one Mrs. Webber came to me about nine days ago. But I have some new information about her that might indicate that she, and even possibly Mrs. Mannstein, are not truly missing. Information from Mrs. Webber."

"I recall the Melton girl. More important, I do want to know the progress of your courtship of Ruthanne."

"Going as planned, General," said Major Plate. "She was clear her information was possibly just gossip about Hortense Melton, who Mrs. Webber says may be found, or at least accounted for, soon. And may have to do with the characters at this gala."

"Good," said Leshoward. "From my superiors in the east, I also have received some information about the guests at the masquerade ball. A new list of who is going to be which character. I have not had time to study it. You said there might be a connection?"

"Who is going to be Helen of Troy?" Plate asked.

"The substitute name provided on the new list is Hortense Melton. The story I'm told is that Hortense Melton went into hiding so she could show up dramatically as Helen of Troy at the gala."

"Exactly as Ruthanne was saying."

"What about connections amongst the parentage of these women. Maybe some of their parents have known each other in the past. I know Thistle Mannstein was an orphan."

"Interesting. Prudence was also an orphan. So she told her husband. But the Melton girl has two living parents."

"Keep them separate. It is best that everyone knows the death of the one woman is isolated from the other two having disappeared. And the missing women are not cause for alarm. All we need right now is to start a panic."

"So you want me to be discreet yet let out specific details?" asked Major Plate.

"Yes, without a doubt."

"Ruthanne told me this facade may have been perpetrated by the Weaving Mistresses."

"Is Ruthanne in this women's group?" Leshoward asked.

"She claims not."

"Good."

"She does say the source of her information is someone in the group who swore her to secrecy. She said there was a rivalry between Thistle Mannstein and Hortense Melton to be Helen of Troy. Hortense could not accept losing the competition. Some fraud was involved in the selection process. There may have been bribes. It is possible the disappearance of both women are connected to who won the right to wear the costume."

"Could the parents have been sent on a wild goose chase to get them out of the way or just left town so as not to be suspected of bribery?" speculated Leshoward.

"I doubt that," said Major Plate. "But it is not impossible."

"So what are we left with? Someone has kidnapped Thistle Mannstein so that Hortense Melton can dramatically emerge from hiding and portray Helen of Troy? This is all about who gets to wear which costume at the ball?" Leshoward asked.

"Social fun and games," said Major Plate.

"If so, this Weaving Mistress group has gone too far. They have forfeited my protection," said the general.

Chapter 29

The morning of the gala dawned with crisp cold windy weather and plenty of sunshine.

Lantern was awake and alone when Major Plate came by looking for her father. The general had already left his house to make arrangements for Lantern to have a carriage from town arrive to transport her to the event that night.

Without inviting him in, she explained the errand and told the soldier his commander would return soon.

"Father will be going hours earlier to supervise preparations. So I will have to go alone."

Her tone was as icy as the wind.

Major Plate took the opportunity to caution Lantern. He told her about the relaxation of concern for the missing women and why. But emphasized that Prudence Horaceton was a confirmed victim.

"The body was identified by its clothing and foul play is expected to be the verdict. Don't open the door to anyone you do not expect."

When Lantern did not react to his statement, he left.

Shortly, there was another knock on the door.

Lantern was annoyed to see a robed woman outside.

"I don't need any more cloth," Lantern called through the door to the Weaving Mistress. "And I have my costume for tonight. It is a little tight but it fits well enough. You must have the wrong location."

"I have a message for the general. I was coming this way so the messenger gave it to me."

Lantern hesitated. She was still alone. She had her gun in her pocket.

Major Plate's warning, fresh in her mind, had been ambiguous.

And she was not sure if she had anything to fear. If Thistle Mannstein had simply been absconded with to make sure some other woman got to play Helen of Troy, all of this cloak and dagger activity was nonsense.

Probably Prudence's husband killed her, thought Lantern.

Soldiers were nearby.

She was safe in Fort Leverage.

It was bright daylight.

Lantern opened the door.

"I'm looking for the general. I have a message," said the woman.

"I'm so sorry. He is not here," said Lantern. "Can I take the message? Perhaps you can just leave it verbally?"

"It's sealed."

The woman awkwardly backed up.

"I will hand it to him personally," said Lantern, still not pulling the door open wide. She put her other hand in her skirt pocket that held the gun. "I'm his daughter."

"Thank you." She handed Lantern the envelope.

Lantern did not glance at the message.

She kept watching through the doorway.

Looking vaguely worried now, the woman continued to make her way down the sidewalk, still backing up a little, but finally turning away.

Lantern shut the door. And locked it behind her.

Chapter 30

"You!"

General Leshoward was headed towards Major Plate's office when he saw a familiar figure approaching him.

He met Abigail Fichton halfway across the courtyard.

"I left a message with your daughter. I coaxed the courier into letting me deliver it so I would have an excuse to see you. I was looking for you," said Abigail. "I wanted to warn you."

"Where have you been? Other women from the colony have gone missing. One has been found dead."

"I'm honored by your concern, General. Listen to me one more time, please."

They began walking instinctively towards the empty section of the barracks where it would be hard for anyone to see them.

"What do you know about these disappearances? What do you know about this death?"

"What do I know? Nothing about that. I want to warn you about this gala. Are you aware of what is going on in France? Anarchists may be involved in worldwide plots. There is danger."

"Even in Kentucky? What danger? Tell me!"

"I paid a high price for helping you many years ago."

"The lives of many men were saved. I was grateful."

"My husband was killed. I lost my social position. I had to leave the church."

"It was a bitter irony to me that the husband of the woman whose words to me saved us from sure defeat was one of the few who perished," Leshoward said.

"My words? Prophecy. It was a prophecy. And I have another one now."

"I prefer to use the word insight. And your husband was a good soldier and a loyal patriot."

"That he died a hero and was elevated in rank, posthumously, has saved me these past years. I was able to sell his land allotment for enough to live on even to this day. Few people pay me for the consulting I do in health matters. But we digress from tonight."

Despite the cool weather, the woman felt a flush of heat and automatically removed her outer garment.

So many years had passed since he had first seen her remove outer clothing. Her gestures had not changed.

She has changed hardly at all, he thought.

"Are you in need of anything?" asked the general.

"No, I must live frugally, but I am not in need. Fabric helps me at times when I need a man's brute strength. And he is a friend."

"A friend?"

"Don't let gossip weigh you down. He's only 19. A boy. I am near middle age. Would you put a young one of teenage years with somebody that much older?" Abigail asked.

"I might," he said, embarrassed inexplicably.

"Of course, many feel it is different when it is the man who is older."

"I do agree about that," said Leshoward.

Abigail did not reply.

"What have you to tell me?"

"I know there are women missing."

It dawned on Leshoward that of the missing women two were married to older men. And both men were coming to this ball tonight without their wives. But if there was any significance to that, he could not grasp it.

"Have you insight? About them?" he asked.

"I've heard rumors, that's all. And also that someone very important is coming," said Abigail.

"Maybe the governor. Maybe someone from Philadelphia. Jefferson has been mentioned. Maybe even George Washington."

"That is my insight. An important personage is the target of a killer. Someone whose life is important to our future."

The general turned pale. Then his temper flared.

"I don't believe it. First, I don't believe any of these famous people are coming. That's as ridiculous as the King of Sweden coming. I do not take any of these rumors seriously. It would be a nightmare to prepare security for such people. I can't guarantee anyone's safety."

"I don't think you need to worry about the security of the King of Sweden. He is not coming. It is our people in danger. Americans."

"That sounds like a prophecy. How can you be sure he's not coming? Is this like your insight on the night of the battle?"

"I don't know," said Abigail unconvincingly.

"There's more to this than insights," said Leshoward with a sudden insight of his own. "You have contacts in Philadelphia."

"Yes, I have contacts," Abigail whispered, turning from him. "I know of treachery. Someone who does not want your tolerant township to succeed."

General Leshoward took hold of Abigail's arm. "You know what is going on here? Who is behind these disappearances, all these rumors, the dead woman? Who does not want our way of life here to continue? It's not witches. I'll never believe that. But you know if someone is betraying us!"

"There is someone here with the old loyalties. But the war was over years ago. How can we keep the old hatreds going? I fear a plot to expose all the old betrayals. If my feeling is right, there may be people hurt. People who have been redeemed by living a good and patriotic life since the end of the war."

"The war may be over but still there is sedition about. How can you be sure anyone loyal to England is now a patriot? You must tell me," Leshoward said.

"If I had more evidence than just my suspicions and the gleaning of my gift, I would name a name. But how can I subject anyone, and their family as well, to the same ostracism and alienation that I have gone through? Unless I am sure they are guilty and also plotting more evil."

"If you go around saying things like you're hundred percent sure the King of Sweden is not coming after we've been hearing rumors about that for months, I cannot protect you if he comes."

"I know he's not coming because on March 16 in Sweden he was shot in an assassination attempt."

"How do you know that?"

"I was informed by a government agent."

"There is an agent here that I do not know about and you do?

112

Are you telling the truth? Or is this more sorcery? More intrigue?"

"You have more enemies than you think," said Abigail. "I am not one of them."

Leshoward bit his lip. "You know why I've protected you all these years?"

"I had my hopes."

"I have shadowed you all these years and keep you protected ever since I came to Fort Leverage. Because of the victory. Because of your vision," Leshoward said.

"I see. In hopes that I might be useful again? That may have come to pass."

"In gratitude. And, yes, in hopes that if there is more war, another treachery, you will lend your gift to us."

"I've told you before. My visions are a gift from God. And I don't control them or summon them like a cup of tea."

"I understand you know about things no one else knows."

"You do believe me about the king."

"Yes, I believe you. What happened? Tell me. Time is pressing. Is the news generally known?"

"Yes. The king is recovering."

"He is one of the characters tonight. Reginald Penberthy is portraying him," Leshoward said. "Foolish nonsense. I see that now. I should have prevented it."

"Yes, I know all about that also."

"If the attempt in Sweden was a minor incident and the king is recovering, we may get some criticism for it being in poor taste, but we can say we didn't know in time. And we will send him our best wishes for a speedy recovery," Leshoward said.

"Yes. I just wanted you to know one more detail. While the assassins were caught and he is recovering, you do need to know the circumstances under which he was shot."

"What were they? How are they pertinent?"

"He was attacked at a masquerade ball."

Chapter 31

The general crossed the courtyard and stopped at Major Plate's office. Abigail had ridden away. All he had was a promise she would reappear at the gala tonight.

If she did know the name of a traitor, he was not going to get it from her yet.

Major Plate wanted to attempt to find Hortense Melton and speak with her immediately.

"Talk to her tomorrow," said the general.

"Don't you think she has a few questions to answer about where she has been?"

"Tomorrow. After the gala. I've just received some news from Europe that I need to discuss with Reginald Penberthy. I'm going to ride out towards his estate in an attempt to catch him on the way. I am sure he has already left. It's probably too late to change anything but I'm going to try to warn him," Leshoward said.

"And my orders?" asked Major Plate.

"Right now I want you to ride out there and check on the Mannstein house. You can return and get Ruthanne later tonight. A carriage is coming for Lantern so I won't be back here. I will come straight from Penberthy's to the Mannstein estate."

Obeying that order, Major Plate arrived at the Mannstein mansion in the early afternoon. He knew Mannstein would be preparing for the ball tonight although he was not technically the host and his attendance was not mandatory considering the personal situation with his wife.

He did not intend to subject Mannstein to any emotional interrogation tonight.

He did have some questions for Naomi but she was not at the main house where she lived.

He might be under instructions not to track down Hortense Melton but Naomi might know something more about the other missing woman, Thistle Mannstein.

He rapped on the servants' door but no one answered.

They were all at the main house, working.

Major Plate tried the door.

Locked.

Maybe Naomi was in the back of the quarters.

He walked around the side.

The backyard at the Mannstein house was on a gentle slope where the detached building took up a tiny space.

When he blacked out, he rolled a short ways down before a manicured bed of roses halted his fall.

"No blame. You've never seen a battlefield," Leshoward said.

"My deepest apologies for passing out, sir,"

Mannstein had directed Major Plate to hold a wet handkerchief to his forehead and keep his neck bent forward to avoid a repeat of his reaction to the sight of the body of Naomi Short.

Naomi had been arranged in pieces on the back lawn.

Her body was carefully positioned by the killer or killers who took her life.

She looked like a life-size strung puppet dismembered at the joints with at least six inches separating each section.

"Looks like she was killed sometime overnight. The servants have all been at the main house preparing for the event," Major Plate had told the general when he arrived.

The general had made quick time in his trip to the Penberthy estate. As he had suspected, Penberthy refused to consider turning around to change costumes. He had his mind set on wearing the costume of the king.

The general felt he had done his duty in reporting the situation and, worried about Abigail's prediction, proceeded as rapidly as possible towards the Mannstein estate.

It was now less than three hours before the gala.

The general was determined this final attempt to disrupt it was not going to succeed.

"It was just like the sheep on the Penberthy lawn," said Plate.

"Exactly the same?" the general asked Plate, as his mind raced with thoughts on how to keep this from becoming known to the arriving guests.

"Only that was a sheep," said Plate.

"To whoever did this, Naomi Short was no more than a sheep," Leshoward said.

General Leshoward ordered the removal of the body immediately, and the area be covered with a fresh layer of dirt.

Henri Mannstein reassured General Leshoward and Major Plate the event would not be compromised despite the murder on his estate that afternoon.

After all, it was just the maide.

Mannstein was still hoping his wife would show up to claim her place as Helen of Troy.

The grave diggers arrived and took the body. Soldiers came with the dirt, shovels, and rakes.

The major was relieved when the general told him the situation no longer required his presence.

Major Plate's focus left Naomi Short mercifully quickly. He appropriated a carriage and called for Ruthanne.

The long awaited gala was about to begin.

Chapter 32

The Mannstein ballroom was indeed ideal for the affair. Guests entered through a double doorway onto a 6-by-9 feet landing, with stairs leading down to the main room.

The doorman would announce each arrival, if asked.

Many people preferred to come through the doors and down the steps without a formal European-style introduction.

Others, already at the party and in the middle of socializing, would be introduced later when the formal dancing began.

"Good evening, Major, Mrs. Webber," said General Leshoward as if he was seeing both people for the first time today.

"I didn't think there would be so many people here this early," Major Plate remarked.

"So far mostly official personnel," said the general. "Just a few guests."

"I feel like an out of place official," Major Plate said.

In the dress uniform of a soldier, he did not look out of place.

"You are to relax and have a good time, Major. I want you and Ruthanne to enjoy yourselves," said Leshoward.

"I think we are going to have a memorable evening," Ruthanne commented.

She was wearing her long red cloak that she claimed represented Little Red Riding Hood.

Major Plate recognized it from when she had first visited his office.

She appeared to be a little embarrassed that she could not afford a real costume.

The room was beginning to fill up.

The substitute Helen of Troy arrived with a little fanfare.

"Mistress Hortense Melton as Helen of Troy."

Not many people looked. Despite being a character that was supposed to be famous for her beautiful face, she was wearing a mask.

She was soon surrounded by Mistresses attempting to serve her.

Neilman Horaceton arrived, smiling. He looked content.

Too content for having proclaimed his wife dead just a short time ago, thought Major Plate.

And the mysterious Hortense Melton has finally shown up.

He tried to recall the miniature portrait of the missing girl but it had faded in his mind.

He had left it in his office.

He could not see her face anyway.

He wandered around to the back of the house and looked out on the back lawn.

It might have been an illusion but it looked like new grass sprouts were already coming up through the dirt.

Chapter 33

"Mistress Lantern Leshoward as Mrs. Deborah Franklin."

Lantern insisted on that exact wording of her announcement.

The carriage sent to pick up Lantern had been perfectly on time and she had enjoyed the quiet ride to the Mannstein estate.

"Good evening, Major Plate," Lantern said formally, not looking at him, but staring straight ahead, as he came up beside her.

Major Plate took Lantern's arm and led her into the center of the room, causing not just a few quizzical looks to be shot their way by the other guests.

"Won't your betrothed be jealous?" Lantern asked.

"I don't know where she is," said Major Plate.

A veiled Weaving Mistress came by with a tray of food. Each took an hors d'oeuvre, thanked the server, and moved slightly away from her so as not to be overheard.

"Do you recognize that one?" asked Major Plate.

"In those veils? I don't recognize anybody," said Lantern.

"Neither do I. Ruthanne is wearing a red robe."

"Have you seen my father?"

"I don't know where he went. I was just talking to him. He is here somewhere."

"I have a sealed message for him from Europe. Delivered by a woman dressed as a Weaving Mistress." Lantern's eyes followed the server as she disappeared into the growing crowd. "I had it in my cloak. Oh, I must've left it at the house."

"I think he already knows what's in the message."

"I did see a woman in red," Lantern said.

"Where?" asked Major Plate.

Lantern reflected, remembering.

"She was going around that corner. It leads to a butler's pantry which has steps up to the kitchen. Maybe she's looking for something different to eat."

"Reginald Penberthy just arrived, I see," said Major Plate.

"Why is he not being announced?"

"Some of the more important guests want to be last. He's

supposed to be the Swedish king. The real king has been injured in Europe in an assassination attempt but he's going to recover. We just found that out. That's what's in the notification. So don't worry about leaving it at your house," said Major Plate.

"All these murders, these missing women. It's getting more and more frightening," Lantern said.

"We're not sure all of the missing women are really missing now. Hortense Melton supposedly is here as Helen of Troy. Thistle Mannstein was to have been Helen of Troy."

"That's the Helen of Troy character over there."

"So I see. I've been looking for her."

Helen of Troy stopped briefly. She pulled her mask off for a second, long enough only for someone staring right at her, like Lantern happened to be, to see her face. Then the mask snapped back in place and she continued.

"Thistle Mannstein?" Lantern asked.

"That's not Thistle Mannstein," said Major Plate. "It must be Hortense Melton. I was hoping Ruthanne would identify her, if I could find Ruthanne."

"Reverend Falldrem is Benjamin Franklin?"

"Louis XVI, the embattled French king. I think the costume was originally meant to be Franklin. But since he died a couple years ago they crossed him off the list. Before she disappeared, Thistle Mannstein handled those details. She turned Franklin's costume into the French monarch. Poor taste to dress up for fun as somebody who just recently passed on."

"But it doesn't matter that all the ancient world characters are dead?" Lantern asked.

"I think they've been dead so long it doesn't matter."

"I wonder where they draw the line. Deborah Franklin died 18 years ago. Surely Mrs. Mannstein would've known that," Lantern said.

"And the French monarch may soon be deposed. Perhaps she didn't get it all done before she vanished."

"Whoever arranged this affair doesn't know anything about what is going on in the world," Lantern said.

"I guess if a person has been dead 20 years it is not so bad but if they have only been dead two, well that's too recent."

"Who is that supposed to be?" Lantern asked.

"Martin Luther," said Major Plate.

"And who is that playing him?"

"Originally it was supposed to be Father McKinsy. Someone's idea of a bad joke or dig at our religious tolerance here in the colony. But he traded with Neilman Horaceton."

"Still investigating his wife's murder? At least that's one missing woman you can account for," Lantern said.

"Yes, not much of a consolation. Just remember what I'm telling you. Somebody killed her. Be careful."

"You're making me nervous. I want to have a good time."

"This should make anybody nervous. Everyone going around in masks like this," Major Plate continued.

"I can tell you about somebody. Now see that Weaving Mistress? The one standing near Hayward? Since we are identifying everyone," Lantern said, pointing, "that's my cousin, Genevieve Brown."

"I never got a chance to meet her. I wish she would take the veil off. Do you and she look anything alike?" asked Major Plate.

"She is more like Jane Penberthy," Lantern said.

The major could not help but feel a pang for his lost love.

Chapter 34

"Mrs. Henri Mannstein as Helen of Troy," intoned a monotonous voice.

Said Lantern to Major Plate, "you just said Helen of Troy was Hortense Melton, not Thistle Mannstein."

Major Plate's eyes automatically went to the landing where an unmasked Helen of Troy stood.

"That is Thistle Mannstein!" Major Plate rushed from Lantern's side and forced his way through the crowd rudely to get to the landing. But before he reached her, Helen of Troy was quickly surrounded by a group of Weaving Mistresses and she disappeared.

Lantern had been looking at Major Plate and failed to see Thistle. But she tried to follow.

In her slim cotton dress, Lantern was able to get through the crowd of more cumbersomely costumed participants, who could not move as fast. But she was unable to catch up with Major Plate.

Henri Mannstein greeted him at the bottom of the landing.

"Thistle has come back," he exclaimed. "I've just been with her. Before she was announced, she was outside. I had a hold of her in the vestibule. But then those women grabbed her and pushed her onto the landing. I heard her name announced. But by the time I caught up with her, they had spirited her away. I saw them take her into a room."

The two men made their way through the crowd.

Several cloaked Mistresses surrounded the room.

Mannstein knocked, then assuming the noise was too loud for Thistle to hear, he pushed the door open.

The room was empty.

"Where is she?" yelled Plate. "I saw her, too."

"She went in here!" Mannstein exclaimed, booming at the top of his lungs. "Oh, she cannot vanish again!"

They went opposite ways in search of Thistle.

Losing sight of Major Plate, Lantern's attention turned back towards the landing as the next arrival prepared to be presented.

Jane Penberthy was making her way towards the landing.

"Reginald Penberthy as King Gustav III of Sweden."

Lantern spotted Hayward Manchester on the landing, standing before the crowd.

"Hayward Manchester as Julius Caesar."

Reginald Penberthy stood right before him. Looking for his wife, he had not yet stepped down. He appeared not to see her. She was behind Hayward and several people stood in her way.

Two Weaving Mistresses approached Penberthy, seemingly to take his cloak and offer refreshments on trays.

Two others stepped towards Hayward Manchester.

The attacks came simultaneously.

From beneath the folds of four robes, the knives came out.

Two were thrust into the flesh of the man dressed as a king.

Reginald Penberthy drew his ceremonial weapon and executed weak imitations of sword fencing movements but it was too late.

The sharp blades had found their mark in his soft stomach.

He felt only cold initially and his legs weakened.

As cognition of impending death showered him with fear, he cried loudly, dropping his sword.

The music stopped.

The crowd fell silent.

Loud moaning from Penberthy as he clutched himself and fell forward competed only with the sound of metal striking metal.

Hayward had been wearing only loose folds of a satin toga. But as the knives came towards him, he flung the excess material aside to reveal a 24-inch short sword.

It was not a ceremonial weapon.

And he made no hesitation and began slashing at the women who came at him.

One turned and ran at the sight of the steel.

Undaunted, the other came straight at him.

After a brief clash of metal, he plunged his blade into her heart.

She fell dead to the floor.

Penberthy's assailants had already run. Manchester's surviving attacker was close behind them.

But while her compatriots became a blur far ahead, making a clean break into the woods, one killer was in front of Margaret Craig, who was apparently coming from the butler's pantry with a tray.

Knife still in hand, shorter than the congressman's wife, the assassin pushed the tray in Margaret's face and with an underhand thrust, plunged the blade of her knife into Margaret's abdomen.

Margaret dropped the tray, raised her arms and stepped back, crying out in a high guttural groan.

Those nearby gasped and drew back as the killer reached after Margaret, grasped her by the waist with one hand and pulled the knife back out of her stomach with the other.

The attacker let go of the taller woman and backed away.

Margaret's arms came down. She bent over forward, grasping her wound. A pain filled moan came from her deep inside.

She doubled up and fell over to the ground on the floor in the butler's pantry.

The killer threateningly held up the dagger for the blood to drip. Turning left, then right, menacingly waving at the crowd.

All got out of her way and so the third assailant made her escape into the dark night.

Back in the main room on the landing, Reginald sprawled face down, softly whimpering, his body heaving as he struggled for breath.

Lantern saw a blank unaware expression on the face of Jane Penberthy.

Her way now unobstructed, she was coming onto the landing in anticipation of being announced.

Puzzled by the confusing sounds and the lack of her name being intoned, Jane was suddenly distracted by the writhing of a man on the floor at her feet.

In horror, she recognized it was her husband.

Reginald ceased moving.

Jane screamed.

Lantern's eyes turned back to Hayward Manchester. He stepped over Thistle Mannstein and went to Jane.

Jane cried out again and would have fallen on top of Reginald if Hayward Manchester had not grabbed her elbows as she began to sink, pulling her back upright.

Chapter 35

A cry of intolerable pain rang above the confused babble of crisis and panic.

Definitely a feminine voice, Lantern first thought it was the attacker stabbed by Hayward reacting in despair to her defeat.

But that woman was dead. Silenced in an instant.

The high-pitched sound was coming from the other direction.

Lantern literally ran into Marchmont Craig, coming from the butler's pantry. He grasped her shoulders, pushed her aside, and kept going into the main room.

"Help! Oh! Please, help! Somebody! Get a doctor!" he called.

Acting on Major Plate's orders, the few soldiers present acted as swiftly as possible, sealing off all exterior exits.

A soldier, fresh from locking the pantry's exit door, ran past Lantern. She turned and followed him a little ways towards the main room.

Most people were standing in shock. Most of the Weaving Mistresses had abandoned the floor sweeping robes.

One retained her costume.

Hayward Manchester was one of the few people moving with any rapidity at all. He handed Jane to Ruthanne Webber who had suddenly, helpfully appeared.

He grabbed the Weaving Mistress still in costume and ripped off her veil.

She did not resist.

Hayward jumped back.

Lantern had a clear look at her face.

Genevieve!

Pushing Hayward away, two soldiers quickly grabbed her arms.

"Lantern!" Major Plate was now yelling.

Father McKinsy and Reverend Falldrem appeared from different directions, came together, and went to the fallen man.

Lantern turned her attention back to Congressman Craig still behind her, shaking and crying.

Lantern started towards the congressman.

"Come with me, hurry," he gasped, running back to the pantry.

Lantern followed and poked her head inside the small room.

A couple of the Weaving Mistresses hovered over a figure prone on the floor not far away.

On her back was the stricken Margaret Craig. She was limp and her eyes narrowed to a slit.

Lantern gasped.

She ran back towards the first violence scene, torn as to which way to go.

By now Ruthanne Webber, Jane Penberthy, and Hayward Manchester were all surrounding Reginald's body.

Nearby, kneeling over the woman with a knife in her chest, Father McKinsy was reciting the Late Rites of the Catholic Church for Thistle Mannstein.

"What's happened over there?" asked Major Plate, going in the direction of the pantry. He grabbed onto Lantern.

Lantern led him into the butler's pantry.

They were suddenly with unknown women who were attempting to help the injured woman on the floor.

"Hold her down," Plate instructed the women. "Don't let her bleed to death. Pull her dress apart to see where she is injured."

That was easy to do, as the dress was already sliced open.

"Lantern, go look for your father," Plate instructed.

Lantern quickly left the room.

Margaret Craig shivered on the floor, every few minutes she pursed her lips and as they were clenched between her teeth, she emitted a high-pitched warbling moan sound, a combination of chalk scratched across a schoolmaster's blackboard and an off-key musical high note.

Reverend Falldrem came in with General Leshoward, and a veiled robed woman.

"We must lift her up, take her upstairs to a bedroom, and put her on a bed," said the preacher.

"NO!" The woman removed her veil. Braced by General Leshoward, Abigail Fichton stood before them.

"That will kill her immediately. You must hold her still, apply pressure to her wound and leave her where she is."

"You would bring this woman in here at this time?" Falldrem demanded angrily. "Why hasn't she been taken away under arrest? Surely she is one of the attackers."

From the cold floor, Margaret's voice warbled another painful broken note.

"We've no doctor. She's the only one here who knows what to do," said Leshoward.

"Surely there are other herbalists in the community. Men who practice medicine as a science, not witchcraft," said Marchmont Craig.

"It's witchcraft when a woman does it, but not a man," said Abigail under her breath.

Margaret Craig attempted to lift her shoulders as she clutched her stomach. Her clothing had been ripped aside. Only the soft slip she had donned, due to her slightly swollen belly not fitting into her ancient world costume, was between her fingertips and her flesh. It was pulled slightly to the side so as not to expose bare flesh.

She fell back.

Drops of blood were seeping very slowly from her wound.

"There are no other herbalists within six hours' time travel of this house," the major told Craig.

"You'd know that if you did not spend all your time in Philadelphia. I know this woman. She can help," said General Leshoward.

Abigail silently knelt beside Margaret.

"Are you not a soldier? Did you not fight along men who fell beside you in battle? You mean to tell me you don't know what to do when you see your comrades fall like this," said Reverend Falldrem. "Have one of your privates give her the same treatment as he would one of your own soldiers."

"Reverend, we are not out on the battlefield."

Leshoward grabbed the preacher and pulled him slightly out the doorway. He put his lips to the preacher's ear so the congressman could not hear the words he next spoke.

"We shot them in mercy on the battlefield when they were in

this condition," Leshoward said.

"What?"

He hissed. "There was nothing else to do."

The minister backed off.

Margaret was still but the awful sound coming through her diaphragm continued.

Abigail left Margaret and came to the doorway.

"Do what you can for her. Try to ease her pain somehow," Leshoward said to Abigail, who stood at Leshoward's shoulder.

"I'm not prepared."

"Surely you can do something," Leshoward said.

Leshoward turned away from the preacher, grabbing Abigail by the shoulders and pushing her further outside the room.

"Ronald, complicated by a coming child, she's beyond help," whispered Abigail.

General Leshoward stiffened.

"On the battlefield we always thought if only there was someone to help. If only we could get them somewhere, to a doctor, to a healer. But we couldn't. So we had to-"

"Ronald, your battlefield instincts were right to ease their pain. Mrs. Craig is going to die. Now, I don't know how long-"

"When there was an objection, or simply no more ammunition and no one had strength to do it by hand- it is never quick- well, there was one time it was over six days..."

Abigail swallowed hard.

Margaret Craig's repetitive anguished sound was significantly louder this time and it penetrated the wall.

The congressman came out the door.

"Do something," Marchmont Craig begged Abigail. "It's getting worse."

All three stepped back inside. There was temporary relative silence as Margaret paused her cries and gasped for breath.

"All right," the preacher conceded. "Mistress, I know not whether you are good or evil but if you can do anything-"

"I have some herbs to ease her pain but I don't have them with me. I would have to go out to my cabin. It may take a little time to prepare them."

"Private Crier, take Mrs. Fichton to her home and return with her as soon as possible," Leshoward said.

Abigail felt a shower of terror. "No, you think I'm a witch. Y'all think I did this. You will take me out to kill me."

"No one will harm you," General Leshoward promised.

"I will only go if you go," she said to Leshoward. Then to the others- "I will only go with the general. He is the only one I trust not harm me."

Leshoward hesitated.

Margaret's next cry was softer but longer.

"Go ahead, man! There's nothing you can do here anyway," said Marchmont Craig. "I'm calm enough to command the situation."

Leshoward looked from Craig, still shaking with desperation in his eyes, to the calm countenance of Major Plate.

Margaret Craig moaned again.

"I leave you jointly in charge with Major Plate," said the general. "As you will need to not leave your wife's side, any orders considering any action within this room must be cleared with him or come from him. Agreed?"

Another slow shrill vocalization of pain.

Higher pitched this time.

And again.

Seconds, not minutes, now separated the cries.

Those kneeling beside her on the hard rock floor completely forgot the pain in their knees.

"Yes. Yes, go! Go and take that witch- mistress, and get back as soon as possible," said the congressman with agitation.

"We can be back quickly if we hurry," said Abigail.

"And if you are a witch and can use any of your witchcraft to help her I pray to God that you do so," said the congressman frantically. "Lord forgive me."

Leshoward took Abigail's arm and led her back out of the hall. He motioned for the major to follow.

"Understand, Ronald, I can only ease her pain until death comes to her. All I can do is pray for her. No other power can help. I know pain makes the hours long-"

"It's not a question of hours, Abigail. She most likely will live on for days." He swallowed hard. "Once with a very strong and muscular young man it was nearly a week."

Abigail was overcome at the despair on his face. She embraced him. He did not push her back.

"The only pain relief she can hope for is death unless you can help," Leshoward said.

As horses were brought to the general and the woman at his side, Leshoward gave firm instructions to Major Plate.

After watching the two people ride away, Major Plate left Crier to stay with Margaret, her husband, the minister, and the ladies who were helping.

As Plate was leaving, Lantern returned saying she could not find her father and Plate informed her he had already come and gone.

Silently holding hands, they watched as events unfolded in the ballroom.

Reginald Penberthy was being carried away.

Jane was following, sobbing, held by Ruthanne Webber.

A sheet covered the attacker felled by Hayward Manchester.

Mannstein knelt nearby, weeping.

A soldier stood guard.

Hayward Manchester had joined the soldiers by the fireplace where they were holding a potential suspect.

Other soldiers were corralling other guests on the opposite side of the room. A few were searching the mansion in case there were other victims.

Suddenly, Lantern clutched Major Plate's arm.

"Do they know who did it? Did they catch the third assassin?" asked Lantern. "The woman who went off with my father. It was she who brought me the message just before the carriage came to get me at the ball."

"They have apprehended someone. She is by the fireplace, next to Hayward Manchester."

"No! Impossible!"

Lantern felt faint for the first time.

She swayed a little bit and Major Plate caught her.

"What is it?" he asked. "What do you know about this woman?"

"She's no assassin!" Lantern cried. "That's Genevieve!"

She abandoned Plate and ran towards her cousin.

Chapter 36

Major Plate did not have time to react before he had to move aside again to let a man carrying another injured person pass.

There was still enough activity and chatter in the room that Margaret Craig's cries only occasionally penetrated and were still blending into the background noise.

The searching soldiers had found another Helen of Troy, wounded and being attended by a Weaving Mistress in the back of the house.

Very much alive, Prudence Horaceton was being carried by her husband across the floor.

He had one arm under her back and the other under her knees. She was clasping his shoulders, holding her head regally as they approached.

When she passed near Major Plate, he reached out his arm and stopped them.

"What happened? Where have you been all this time? Tell me as much as you can," said Major Plate.

Prudence Horaceton appeared to faint in Horaceton's arms.

"My wife is been through a great ordeal, Major," said Neilman Horaceton. "She was held hostage for days, then attacked this night. A minor knife wound, a scratch on her thigh, fortunately it was bound well by a kind Weaving Mistress. The bleeding has stopped. I am taking her home."

Major Plate had no choice but to watch Prudence be carried away.

As they disappeared, Lantern returned to his side. The soldiers had prevented her from talking to Genevieve.

"What will happen to Genevieve?" Lantern was asking.

"She might be arrested. I don't know."

"Oh, Lord," Lantern said.

"Come on, let me take you home. Your father asked me to."

"What about Ruthanne Webber?"

Major Plate had forgotten about Ruthanne. He looked around in surprise.

Ruthanne was no longer in view. Hortense Melton was also unaccounted for.

"I did see the woman in red with Jane Penberthy," said Lantern.

"Ruthanne must have gone home with Jane," said Major Plate with relief.

Manchester approached with a request.

While he considered the consequences, Plate asked Manchester to check on Marchmont Craig, still attending Mrs. Craig in the kitchen.

More hurried activity distracted everyone.

Even Henri Mannstein temporarily abandoned his vigil at the body of his dead wife. Father McKinsy went to his side.

"Who is that?" Lantern asked, as two other soldiers came out from the depths of the house with another body draped across a door panel removed to serve as a gurney.

This victim was covered in a sheet to the neck.

The face of a very pale woman, her eyes closed, was all that was visible.

"That is your servant, Emilia!" Plate exclaimed.

"She was stabbed," said one of the soldiers.

"Take her to a bedroom upstairs," said Henri Mannstein, as he came to see the victim. "She can be cared for here."

"There is absolutely no way I am leaving," Lantern declared to Plate. "I am needed here."

She and the priest followed Emilia upstairs.

Henri returned to Thistle.

Hayward Manchester reported the congressman was still extremely distraught, nearing incoherency. But the reverend was still calm and the scene under control.

Also deciding to remain, Major Plate gave new orders to the soldiers holding Genevieve. Then he conferred with Private Crier quietly, giving him orders to follow the Horaceton couple home, a short list of questions, and instructions to return with the answers as soon as possible.

Delay had let Hortense Melton slip away again.

Plate was not going to make the same mistake twice.

Chapter 37

Two hours later, Emilia's condition had stabilized. The bleeding had stopped but she remained unconscious. Lantern and Father McKinsy were with her. He had sent for nuns from the convent to help. They were on their way.

Hayward Manchester had left and returned.

Private Crier had also come back and talked for some time with the major.

General Leshoward arrived at that time with news.

"Reginald Penberthy is dead," he confirmed. "Abigail Fichton has returned with herbs for the pain for Mrs. Craig. Have we identified the attackers?"

"It is unclear. Two women have been named besides the dead assassin," Major Plate summarized for the general.

But he did not say names and Leshoward did not ask.

Reverend Falldrem remained with Margaret as did her husband.

Henri Mannstein remained with his wife's body.

All guests had been spoken to and sent home.

"Horaceton claims Prudence was forced into a Helen of Troy costume by her captors and then taken to the gala." Major Plate was narrating this scene to the general and Hayward Manchester in the empty ballroom. "I had a solder follow them home to question them."

The three men sat in the center of the room, within summoning distance of either injured woman.

"Horaceton says Emilia confronted his wife when she tried to change out of the costume in a small room upstairs. He saw Emilia and Abigail Fichton attacking her. Horaceton subdued Emilia and wounded her. Abigail fled," the major added.

"Abigail Fichton was not involved," said the general.

"So Prudence was trying to change out of her costume," Major Plate repeated thoughtfully. "Just because two other women were dressed the same? Or because the costume was forced on her."

"Both. Doesn't that make sense?" asked Hayward.

"What was she going to change into?" asked Major Plate.

"Her cloak?" Hayward suggested.

"She didn't have one, did she?" asked Plate. "We don't know."

"This looks like a well-planned conspiracy," Hayward said. "I, for one, do not intend to let an innocent woman take the blame."

"Who? Has some other innocent been accused?" asked Leshoward.

"Father, it's Genevieve."

Lantern came downstairs and took the major's arm.

The general looked at Major Plate quizzically.

"My soldiers have found anarchist materials in French in a print shop where your niece has done work," said Major Plate. "I had them check out the shop yesterday."

"Without my authority? All right. So where do we stand?" the general asked.

"Emilia is still clinging to life," Lantern reported.

"Hortense Melton has disappeared again," Major Plate said.

"This is all impossible! And to accuse Genevieve! As far as we know it was any of these women," Leshoward said. "Or all of them."

"No. There were four killers. The other women did nothing but these four women had no hesitation when they made their moves," said Plate.

"So we narrow it down to four women," Leshoward said.

"We thought the three attackers that survived left the premises. But apparently, all they did was go around and mix back in with the other similarly dressed women," said Hayward.

"Several have bloodstains on their clothes, claiming the killers brushed against them and escaped," Plate said.

"So you think the perpetrators simply did their best to get blood on the other women's clothing, ran out, then they came back to blend in?" Leshoward asked.

"So could be any of them, or they could all be in on it. Or just some of them as part of the organization. Depends on how much of a conspiracy it was," Plate said.

"Or just the act of maniacs working together," Hayward said.

"And the attacks on the other people? Then how can you suspect Genevieve more than the others?" asked the general.

"The pamphlets in her possession," said Plate.

"They could have been planted," Leshoward said.

"I had not thought of that. In a conspiracy, that would make sense," Plate admitted.

"Can we really explain anything that has happened?" asked the blacksmith.

"The attack on Margaret Craig can be explained. She got in the way of one of them escaping," said Major Plate.

"Good, seems obvious," Leshoward said. "Where is my niece?"

"I sent her to your house under guard," said Plate.

"I took her myself," said Hayward.

"Good. That was a good decision," said the general.

"What next?" asked the major.

"Try to talk personally to Horaceton, officially. See what he knows. Why did he identify Prudence as being the dead woman? God be pleased to let Abigail's potions work on that poor woman."

One of Margaret's screams had been loud enough to penetrate the conversation from the distance.

Everyone held their breath a moment, waiting to hear another, but it was faint.

Hayward abruptly shifted.

"I am going home. Keep my short sword and dispose of it as you like. I don't like memories. I have no use for a weapon after it has killed," said Hayward.

No one objected.

Lantern embraced him before he left.

Plate and Leshoward resumed talking.

"We had considered the Mannsteins pretty much above suspicion. Thistle's vanishing and reappearance are still our concern," Leshoward said.

"Even though she is dead?" asked Major Plate.

There was a noise on the landing.

The priest had arranged for a stretcher to take the body of Thistle Mannstein away. Hayward Manchester's short sword was still visibly causing a risen mound in the sheet covering her as she was lifted by the grave diggers and carried out of the room.

Chapter 38

"It seems clear Thistle Mannstein was one of the assassins. Numerous witnesses saw her attack Hayward and he killed her almost instantly. No way could someone have switched places with an innocent woman between the time of the attack and the time Hayward struck in self-defense," said Major Plate.

Henri Mannstein had accompanied his wife's body to the convent for burial.

Leshoward took complete control of the mansion. He seized the contents of Mrs. Mannstein's desk.

With no way of knowing which of the women were the killers, everyone went back home with two exceptions.

Genevieve was at the fort with her uncle and Lantern. Ruthanne went to stay with Reverend Falldrem and his wife.

Neither the print shop nor the vacated Melton home was seen fit for a woman alone under these circumstances.

Back at his home office, Leshoward locked Thistle Mannstein's papers in his file cabinet.

The general then sought Major Plate, dismissing the other soldiers for the time being.

"You are sure about Mrs. Mannstein?" General Leshoward asked Plate, once the two men were alone. "I didn't see any of the killings. I was conferring with Mrs. Fichton. She was with me during the attacks. So Horaceton was either lying or truly mistaken about her."

"Yes, sir. I did see, or rather hear, the attacks on the men."

"That sequence of events seems to be less of a mystery than the violence among the women. And the other facets of their behavior. It appears you were right. There was much more to the Weaving Mistress organization than an exercise of democratic capitalism. I want to know the whole story before these people are mourned and buried," Leshoward said.

"You would still like to know the story behind the disappearance of Thistle Mannstein? Even if she was guilty."

"Indeed I would."

"So would I. And what about the woman identified as Prudence? And Naomi's murder?" Major Plate asked.

"Still a priority. Obviously, the schoolmaster made a mistake. Or?"

"Or lied."

"He only had clothing to go by," Leshoward said. "That is why you need to talk to them first. Find out where Mrs. Horaceton has been and why she returned on the eve of this affair. And exactly how she got into a scuffle with my housemaide. If you conduct that inquiry, then I cannot be accused of bias. I will concentrate on the Mannstein woman. The death of the maide must be connected. I will talk to Henri myself."

"Yes, sir," said Major Plate, not wanting to point out to his superior that any inquiry into Henri Mannstein by the general might also be suspect.

Chapter 39

"You were in the Weaving Mistress group?"

"I had joined. To try to make a little money."

Less than 36 hours later, Major Plate sat on the couch in Prudence Horaceton's modest house. She sat adjacent to him. Her husband stood behind her, hovering protectively.

"I feel relief and happiness that this ordeal is over and I have finally come home to be with my husband. So what more do you want to know?" asked Prudence. "I didn't know where I was until I escaped. I was blindfolded for days."

"How did you get away?" asked Major Plate.

"They brought me to the gala after making me put on the Helen of Troy costume. As soon as I arrived, somebody grabbed me, one of the Weaving Mistresses. Emilia."

"Were you the costumed person announced as Hortense Melton?"

"That was not me!"

"You say your assailant grabbed you?"

"Right, and pulled me into a pantry. She and another woman locked the door and told me I had to undress since Thistle was the rightful Helen of Troy. I was just stunned."

"You did not scream for help?" asked Major Plate.

"I refused their demand and was attacked!"

"How did you fight her off? Did you have a weapon that was part of your costume?"

"No. We struggled out of the pantry and someone pulled us apart. I became faint and the next thing I knew, Neilman was there to save me."

"Did you know about the other people attacked?" asked Plate.

"No! I just heard these terrible screams of pain. Emilia was yelling in my ear up close at the same time. How is she, by the way? Will she live? What story has she told you? And Margaret Craig, I understand, was the source of the terrible screams."

"She is still alive?" asked Neilman.

He had retracted his claim that Abigail Fichton was the second attacker, claiming he could not identify her positively.

"You wounded Emilia on her shoulder. She was not found in the chaos for a long time and lost a lot of blood. She is not conscious yet. We do not know if she will live to wake up. Margaret Craig is dying slowly, suffering greatly. There is no hope. She is bravely facing certain death."

"My goodness, Mrs. Craig is awake? Who is with her? What is she saying?" asked Prudence.

"Volunteers from the Weaving Mistress group are with her. And most of the time her minister. She infrequently voices a concern for her baby. Otherwise it takes all her strength to cope with the pain."

Prudence blinked. "She was expecting a baby? I didn't know that. My goodness! And no hope for her recovery!"

And the expression on her face showed genuine distress.

Chapter 40

"I want to confess."

It was some time before anyone acted on Margaret's words.

The herbs Abigail had brought had not relieved the pain Margaret Craig felt within her belly but they had changed it.

At first, the substances, combined with the wine contributed by Father McKinsy, had brought a brush of optimism with relaxation.

Margaret hallucinated for a short wonderful time, fantasizing that she was in labor, her pains productive childbirth agony, her baby about to be born.

Then her brain cruelly adjusted her body's tolerance to the potion and the wine ran out.

She became fully coherent again.

The reality of the cause of the pain returned.

She was bearing it.

Still helpless on the floor, excessive movement meaning death, fires had been lit to help keep her warm. Blankets were tucked around her.

Once lucidity returned permanently, she would allow nothing save the pink stained silk garment she had worn since the morning of the ball to remain on top of her wound.

If someone dared to try to place another coverlet over the spot, she cried until she could fling it aside or someone removed it.

If they left her alone, there was no need to hold her down.

There was very little blood, almost none fresh.

Her abdomen was swelling a little more each hour.

She remained as immobile as she possibly could. She was now dramatically more still than at first, due to the help of the herbs.

All agreed moving her would still be fatal. Some said it would be merciful to lift her up and let the blood flow out.

No one was willing to take the responsibility to do that.

They decided against traditional bleeding at the wrists. It would be futile.

Her attenders changed. It had gotten so that no one could stand to be in the room for significant periods.

No one felt they could do anything except sit with her.

Some sat near her on the floor. Others in chairs looking down.

She ignored them all, focusing on her injury, asking only twice if the baby inside her was intact and unharmed.

She was assured it was.

There was so little blood from her wound.

No one dared talk very much.

They were afraid she might give some indication that she believed she could survive and they would have to truthfully explain that she could not.

They wondered if she planned in her mind to endure this agony another five or six months.

The biological will to live in face of the cognition of certain death overwhelming the pregnant woman.

Or were the moments of hope in her face when the word baby was whispered, mere delusions?

Outside the deathwatch chamber, several people advocated a higher dose of the herbs provided by Abigail Fichton.

Privately Abigail had confided to Leshoward that she dared not give Margaret a higher dose of the herbs lest she became responsible for the knifed woman's death herself.

There was no way Leshoward was going to advocate Abigail take such a risk.

He wanted no one to carry the guilt he hid within himself, justified and merciful his battlefield actions may have been.

The dying woman's agony brought it all back to him.

In the middle of the second day, mercifully for those who attending her, especially her husband, Margaret had ceased shrilly warbling in agony at regular intervals.

The verbal expression of her suffering came only occasionally, sometimes as much as a quarter of an hour apart, intervals seemed to be growing longer.

It mostly took the form of a groan of mourning.

As the second day progressed, most of the time she was calm, concentrating on taking deep breaths staring at the ceiling, and occasionally whispering to those next to her, without turning her head or making any type of eye contact.

Then she repeated her unexpected dramatic statement.

Reverend Falldrem was then summoned to her side.

Falldrem knelt down on the floor.

He gently took one of her hands into his and bent her elbow, slightly elevating her palm.

"I want to confess, I want forgiveness," she gasped. It was several minutes and numerous deep breaths before she could do anything except gaze vacantly at the ceiling.

Falldrem held her hand tightly and prayed silently. His knees began to ache.

"Confess," she said, finally.

"What do you want to confess my dear?" He tried to keep any impatience out of his voice. "Confess to your Savior, not me."

Another deep breath.

Everyone braced, expecting another shrill warbling moan but none came.

"I killed Hayward Manchester."

She said these words sharply and audibly so that everyone in the room could clearly understand them.

Falldrem eased his grip in confusion and she snatched her hand from his, clutched her wounded stomach tightly once more, and took another deep breath.

"The Lord forgives all sins-" Falldrem began almost instinctively, automatically.

Margaret gave a sharp cry and sat up almost at a right angle.

Then she let out her last shrill sound of betrayal.

And fell back, in pain no more.

Chapter 41

"But Hayward Manchester is not dead."

General Leshoward had not been in the room when Margaret died so he had not heard her final words. He was having trouble believing them.

"No, she must've been delirious," he told Plate in the latter's office that evening.

Major Plate had not been there either.

"Obviously she meant to say she saw who killed Hayward Manchester or she knew who was going to try to kill him. She was dying. She got confused," Leshoward said.

"Agreed," Plate said.

"Thank heavens, the poor woman no longer suffers. We have to figure out what has happened. We can't put every woman that was part of this organization in jail. But we can't let any of them go either. Three of them are murderers or would-be murderers," Leshoward said.

"Agreed," Plate said.

"For what it's worth, soldiers searching the mansion found two discarded Weaving Mistress robes. They have an abandoned Helen of Troy costume identical to the one Thistle Mannstein died in, under her cloak that is, and to the one Prudence Horaceton was wearing," Leshoward said.

"Really? Hortense's gown?" Major Plate's eyebrows rose.

"Maybe. We do know Thistle Mannstein covered her costume with the cloak. Apparently they all wore costumes under those cloaks. Or were supposed to."

"Wasn't Margaret Craig wearing only undergarments underneath her robe?"

"The congressman explained that. Her costume had ceased to fit her in her new condition. She wasn't the only one. Some of the other women had gained a little weight since they were issued their clothes," Leshoward said.

"You mean several of these women were wearing nothing but the robe and their undergarments?" asked Major Plate.

144

"Yes."

"I'm sorry I missed that search detail. What else?" Major Plate asked.

"That's about it. Except- "

"Yes?"

"Major Plate, how do you feel about talking with Jane Penberthy?"

Major Plate blinked at the question. Feelings usually did not enter into such decisions in a soldier's duty.

"If it will help," Major Plate said.

"It has been mentioned that she might reveal something to you that would not come out otherwise, considering your relationship in the past," Leshoward said.

"She's not under suspicion, is she?" That idea was incredible to Major Plate. "How is she?"

"Bearing up well. She had not been with him very long."

"That makes it worse for her, I think," said Major Plate. "Anyway, just let me know."

"You were right about one thing and I was wrong."

"Sir?"

"You should have immediately spoken with Hortense Melton as soon as Ruthanne told us she had returned," Leshoward said.

"No trace of her has been found?"

"Nothing except the discarded Helen of Troy costume."

"Are we to assume that she was one of the attackers and she got away?" asked Major Plate.

"Very likely. The Helen of Troy costumes were perfect to disguise one of those daggers," Leshoward said.

"So there were three Helen of Troys," mused Major Plate.

"It was the only one of the old world costumes that was designed with both the mask and a veil. It was easy to move in. It was easy to take off. It was easy for that robe to disguise it."

"We're sure that the woman who was announced as Hortense Melton was in reality Hortense Melton?" asked Major Plate.

"We're not sure of anything at this point. We're only sure that one of the Helen of Troys was Thistle Mannstein," Leshoward said.

Both had been vividly picturing how Manchester's sword had penetrated the fabric of both the robe and the tight bosom portion of the otherwise loose fitting gown representing Helen of Troy.

"It stands to reason that Prudence Horaceton was one of the killers," Leshoward said.

"Not necessarily. She had a letter that she won the lottery to actually be Helen of Troy. The theory is she was abducted to prevent her from being there so the assassins could use that disguise."

"Nobody saw any of the Helen of Troys without their masks," Leshoward said.

"Somebody did," Major Plate said excitedly. "Sir, have I you authorization to proceed in confidence?"

"As you might have guessed, I have been conferring with the leaders of the colony. Reverend Falldrem, Father McKinsy have been advising me. Henri Mannstein and Marchmont are too distraught to contribute much. But I am loathe to leave them out of our discussions," Leshoward said.

"Agreed," Plate said.

"Yet I do want you to proceed, Major, with ideas of your own that you may have. You need not clear them with me. Just report any results as you feel needed to the authorities in Philadelphia. And I will also keep you informed. Messengers with the news of what has happened here are on their way to Philadelphia and Richmond and New York. What the consequences will be, I do not know. But regardless we must find out who else wielded these killing blades if we find out nothing else."

"Yes, sir," Plate said.

Consequences soon became apparent. In record time communications yielded replies to the news of what had happened in Kentucky. Military authorities were coming personally to review the events with the general.

Their initial comments were not supportive. But they had a long way to travel before they could make an impact on the investigation.

It looked like Leverageton would have important national visitors after all.

Chapter 42

Major Plate proceeded to follow the general's orders. He put a plan in action.

His first step was a conference with Lantern.

"The night of the gala I told you I thought I saw Hortense Melton."

"Yes, I remember," said Lantern.

"I want you to draw that face for me immediately. The girl you saw when she pulled her mask off for that few seconds at the party. Also draw any faces you saw at the secret meeting we stumbled upon in the woods. You did see faces that night?"

"Just one or two. That's a fairly tall order," Lantern said.

"Can you do it? I especially want to know who was in that Helen of Troy costume."

"Yes, I can do it. It will take some time. Are you saying that assassin was not Hortense Melton?"

"I don't know. It might have been. I realize now I just assumed it was her," Plate said.

"She's gone missing again and you think she's dead?"

"She may yet be dead. If you saw her at the ball, someone else might have recognized her also."

"She only had the mask off a second," Lantern said.

"Sometimes that's all it takes. She may be an innocent victim in all this. She might have gone into hiding for fear of her life. It's possible the reason that they lured her away from Fort Leverage was because they didn't want her wearing the costume. It's possible her coming back disrupted all their plans. Or maybe she's one of the assassins. The ringleader with the audacity to use her own name and get away."

"So the costumes were some type of identification of the killers," Lantern said.

"Maybe," Major Plate said.

"I'll work on the drawings. The Helen of Troy- it will take me some time having to do it from a brief flicker of a memory like that. But I will do the best can," Lantern said.

"I need to see your cousin now," said Major Plate.

Lantern frowned.

"Trust me. It is important," said Major Plate.

Lantern gazed into his eyes.

"What good would questioning her further do?"

"Believe me, it is in your cousin's best interest if I question her. And your father's."

"Very well."

Lantern summoned Genevieve from her upstairs room and left her alone with Major Plate in the parlor.

"I'm sure there is nothing left for me to tell you," said Genevieve.

"Only the truth about what you are really doing here," said Plate.

Chapter 43

A few days after the violence, tension remained high.

Rumors ran wild that an important personage from Philadelphia would arrive to take over the colony and disrupt the positions of every local official.

General Leshoward's fate as leader of the colony seemed bleak.

The time frame was moved up for the wedding of Ruthanne and Major Plate. Until that point in time, Ruthanne would continue to stay with Reverend Falldrem. Then she would move into the small office/bedroom where the major lived in the fort.

Talk was the larger house inside the fort would soon be available.

"Your father is refusing to arrest or detain anyone. You must talk to him. The government communiques are now coming straight to me, unofficially as yet, but effectively bypassing your father. That is not a good sign," said Major Plate to Lantern, as they sipped tea.

He had slipped her a message and told her to make a pretense to come into town, meet him and act as if they had met by chance.

They were in the small tea parlor across the street from the printer's shop.

The establishment was empty except for the proprietor who kept his distance at a gesture from the soldier.

Major Shears Plate did not want his conversation with Lantern Leshoward overheard.

"A tenet of our democracy is that you are innocent until proven guilty," Lantern said.

"That looks fine on paper but when someone's life is at stake, it is harder to adhere to the ideal."

"He told me the only person he has any evidence against is Neilman Horaceton. But not enough for an arrest," Lantern said.

"What evidence does he have?" asked Major Plate.

"Horaceton came to the ball dressed in one of the costumes that was up for lottery," Lantern said. "According to Thistle Mannstein's records, he never entered the costume contest."

"The character lottery was fixed," said Major Plate.

"Fixed?"

"Yes. Which people were selected to be which character was supposed to be some type of code for some type of clandestine operations during the war."

"How did you find that out? How did I get a character? I was a child during the war," Lantern said.

"Your cousin arranged your costume for you," said Major Plate.

"Oh. She told you that?"

"You had no idea she was any part of this organization?"

"We had no idea this organization was dangerous. They lived among us. Existed under my father's protection. Do you know what all this is about?" Lantern asked.

"Some," Major Plate admitted. "I don't know the details. But there exists in the world a group of people who do not want our democracy to succeed. They hold with no government, not by king, congress, or religion. But they use the misguided religious, such as those who believe in witchcraft, and the misguided loyalists, who serve a king or emperor before God, as a means to their end. And they achieve their ends by killing, believing constant disruption by bloodshed will eventually bring down any government."

"Genevieve is not a member of such an organization. She is not a killer," Lantern insisted. "What's going to happen?"

"Your father's being accused of protecting Genevieve because she's his niece. She has never told you anything?" asked Major Plate.

"She knew about your betrothal to Ruthanne before you did," Lantern said.

"Did she say anything else about Ruthanne?"

"No. I don't think that you have to worry that your betrothed is involved in this."

"It is more important than ever that you draw the faces of the women you saw in the woods that night," Major Plate said.

Lantern opened up her sketchpad. She refrained from telling Plate it was Genevieve she had followed to the woods that night. She pulled out two sketches.

"I finished partly. This woman was at the meeting. And this is the woman who left the message the day of the gala," she said.

Plate studied the detailed sketches.

Lantern could see by the look on his face Plate recognized one.

"Who is it?"

"I think this is Abigail Fichton. Don't you remember her from the ball? I had never seen her before that night," said Major Plate.

"Yes. I've never seen her except for a few moments but I think you're correct. I think it could be her," Lantern said.

"I'm sure."

"Then why does not Father arrest her?" Lantern asked in frustration.

"He says he was with her at the time of the attacks."

"And this is the drawing of the other woman whose face I saw clearly. They called her the Mistress Superior," Lantern said.

"Thistle Mannstein. Why didn't you tell us this before?"

"I had never actually met her. I never saw her face at the ball. I never looked at the woman Hayward Manchester killed at the ball. I was with others- you, Margaret, Emilia- the whole time," Lantern said.

"What about that other drawing I asked you to do?" asked Major Plate.

"I'm still working on it. I'm untrained at this, you know. That image was much harder to do. Seeing her, it was just like a flash of lightning."

"Thistle Mannstein is the only killer we are sure of. Besides your cousin, the only other named suspect is Emilia."

"And you know that Emilia's run off?" Lantern asked.

"My God, no! The general claims she's in seclusion at your house. Still recovering from her wound," said Major Plate.

"When we got up yesterday morning, she was gone," Lantern said.

"He hasn't reported it. This is serious. He could lose more than just his rank and position over this."

"I may have an idea where she's gone. But I've no way to go look for her myself," Lantern said.

"For heaven sakes tell me where!"

"I suspect she is with Fabric. Oh, yes! She must be. With all this going on I had forgotten about that romance."

"So had I. I will ride out there this afternoon."

"What will you do if you find her there?" Lantern asked.

"Bring her back to the fort, of course. And him along with her. Do you know how or why Emilia got involved with these people?" asked Major Plate.

"They promised Emilia if she became a part of their organization, they could get freedom papers for Fabric," Lantern said.

"That is what they do. I'm sure they promised many things to many people. We can assume Mrs. Mannstein was not their only operative. Until we know for sure, everyone involved with this gala is suspected. Authorities in Philadelphia want answers."

"Are you in contact with someone from Philadelphia?"

"Yes and don't ask me any more than that. I am just a soldier taking orders. And there is one more thing."

"What else can there be?" Lantern asked.

"Jane Penberthy. It's now being said among the soldiers and probably among the townspeople also," said Major Plate.

"What's being said?"

"The general is spending a great deal of time consoling Jane Penberthy."

"No, I can't believe that. There's nothing between my father and Jane Penberthy. It was you who courted her," Lantern said.

"In what seems another world, yes. Jane has no interest in me now."

"Of course not. You're betrothed to Ruthanne," Lantern said.

"Right. Yes. I'm risking a court martial for telling you this. But the general has been like a father to me. Try to talk to him. Tell him he's got to put these women that are under suspicion in some kind of detention. Ask him what's going on with Jane Penberthy. If all this were settled, I suppose a union between him and Jane might not be that farfetched. But it's a bad idea right now. I am sure military officials are on their way here as we speak."

Major Plate rose from the table and indicated to the tea parlor owner he could open up again.

"Can you get back to the fort on your own?" asked Major Plate.

"Of course," Lantern said.

"I'm going out to the cabin. If Emilia is there, I'll bring her back to the fort. Genevieve said you gave her some papers to hold. She asked you to bring them or have them available if you were keeping them at the house. Keep in mind they can be used against her."

"I guess everything has to come out now," said Lantern, feeling grief for Emilia's and Fabric's situation.

"If she's not there, I'll return anyway. My betrothal to Ruthanne has complicated this situation," said Major Plate.

"Isn't she staying with the reverend and his wife?" Lantern asked.

"They only have a two-room house. Hardly room for themselves. Our wedding has been moved up. In fact, the ceremony is scheduled for tomorrow tonight," said Major Plate.

"I had no idea," Lantern said.

Her grief became introspective.

"We are supposed to be at your house tomorrow afternoon for a wedding reception that would include you and the general and a requisition of wine for the soldiers. Ruthanne knows no one here except for Genevieve."

"You are not to go to a ceremony at the church?"

"It was just going to be a private service with myself and Ruthanne and the pastor at the church. Your house was going to be the most convenient location for a small celebration after the ceremony. The church is so far, I won't have time to do that now. May I send a message to Ruthanne and Reverend Falldrem to meet me at your house and we can just be married there?" asked Major Plate.

"Just have the ceremony there?"

"Yes. In the morning, as soon as we can get everything arranged and everyone there."

"I don't see why not," Lantern said.

"That will give me time to go and get Emilia before her disappearance causes real trouble."

"So this is our last meeting?" Lantern asked.

"I don't see why we can't be friends even after my marriage."

"That is not the way of the world," Lantern said.

"Ask your father if you can't marry one of the soldiers, or another soldier who could be brought from Philadelphia or someplace and we could all be friends."

Plate had a strange look on his face.

"I will never marry," said Lantern.

Chapter 44

Lantern rode somberly towards home.

A late spring snow fell unexpectedly.

Just a light dry dusting to give the land a demur beauty.

Her mind was torn between emptiness at her relationship with Shears Plate coming to an end and what excuses she would give to her father for again meeting the soldier without permission.

She was distressed that Fabric and Emilia would not be able to have a life together once the papers Genevieve forged were handed over.

She also worried about her father's future.

That worry turned to fear as soon as she entered the house.

Even before she called out, she decided no one was there.

Then she found a simple note from her father.

"Do not worry. Had to make an unexpected trip and will be back early tomorrow," was all it said.

Plate did not return with Emilia and Fabric, so Lantern ended the day as she had begun- alone.

Feeling stunned and betrayed, she spent a long night, sleeping downstairs on the couch.

She slept fitfully but did get some rest.

Rising early, there was nothing to do but prepare for the wedding as best she could. She soon had the parlor area spotless and food divided out in the kitchen to prepare as soon as the wedding party arrived.

She spent the rest of the time in prayer until she heard the sound of a carriage. Reverend Falldrem and Ruthanne were climbing out as Lantern swung open the door.

At the same moment a more simple wagon arrived carrying Major Plate, Fabric, Emilia, and an unexpected person- Father McKinsy.

"They were not at the cabin. I had to go all the way to the convent to get them," Major Plate told Lantern.

"I intend to see to it that Emilia is not made the scapegoat for the tragedy at the masquerade ball," said the Catholic priest.

"My father would never make a scapegoat out of anyone," said Lantern.

"Your father is not going to have anything to do with this," said the cleric. "I have just heard the news that he has gone off with Jane Penberthy."

"That's not true!" Lantern said.

"They were seen. Her with her golden hair flying out of the carriage."

"He must be with my cousin, Genevieve. She has light brown hair that looks golden in bright light," Lantern said.

"There's one way to find out," said Major Plate. "I'll send one of the soldiers to the Penberthy estate and see if she is gone also."

As he spoke, Ruthanne shed her outer robe, revealing a simple off-white cotton and lace wedding gown. She carried a handsome leather bag, large enough to hold a few personal items and a change of clothes. From it she pulled a white garment and she unfolded a net veil topped with a small bow.

She arranged the garment around her shoulders, it was a waist length satin cape.

"Would you help me with the veil?" she asked Lantern.

"Of course."

"Thank you," Ruthanne said stiffly.

"The ceremony will have to wait until General Leshoward gets back," said Major Plate.

"Why?" asked the preacher.

"We have witnesses," said Major Plate. "But the ceremony has to wait for the general to come back. This is his house."

"I agree, Shears," said Ruthanne. She went to stand beside him. Their manner towards one another was cordial. They did not touch.

At that moment, the staircase door came open and Genevieve entered.

Everyone gasped. She was in no way wearing traveling clothes. She wore a full length robe of pale yellow with fragile embroidery as if she had just risen.

"You've been here all night?" asked Major Plate.

"Of course, where else would I be?" Genevieve asked.

"Where's my father?" Lantern asked.

"He hasn't returned yet?" Genevieve asked.

"You must have been hiding," said Lantern to Genevieve.

"I was asleep upstairs all night," said Genevieve innocently.

"You didn't go with him? Has he gone off with Jane Penberthy?" asked Major Plate.

"Jane Penberthy?" Genevieve's eyes widened.

"That's the rumors," Lantern said.

"No, I don't know anything about where he might've gone."

"He left a message saying not to worry. I assumed you were with him. I thought I was alone all this time. I had no idea you were in the house."

"A messenger did arrive yesterday with a letter from my uncle addressed to Lantern. I was told not to give it to her until this morning. I overslept," Genevieve said to Major Plate.

Genevieve pulled an envelope from inside her robe.

"It was sealed so I didn't open it. I assumed it was personal."

"Open it and read it, Lantern," said Major Plate.

Lantern took the envelope and broke her father's seal. At first, she spoke softly and then her voice strengthened as more words came.

" 'My Dear Lantern,

Please forgive the subterfuge in the note I left at the house. I did not dare confide my plans on a piece of paper that might fall into the wrong hands. I will be returning with a special guest later tonight. You know how we had hoped for an important personage to come to Fort Leverage for the ball. While this visit will be late, it will be no less important. We will entertain Thomas Jefferson overnight and for part of the next day. We will be there in time for the wedding of Major Plate and Ruthanne.' "

"My goodness," said Genevieve. "He expected us to read that much earlier. Now we are pressed for time to prepare."

The excitement of the great statesman's impending presence overwhelmed the fears concerning exactly what implication his visit might have. But in the back of their minds they all thought this was the end of life in Kentucky as they knew it.

A good part of their lives might be behind them with uncertain futures. Still, the impressive idea that Jefferson would soon be in the room with them was breathtaking.

"I suppose that means we can expect them at any moment," said the reverend.

"I had better change. Anyone know if it is okay to wear dark green? That is the only color satin dress I have. Will it be all right?" Genevieve asked.

No one replied.

"I'll assume it is acceptable." Genevieve went back upstairs.

Ruthanne looked dazed. At that moment, the soldier sent to find out about Jane Penberthy returned with the widow.

"You were not meant to bring her here," Major Plate snapped at the soldier.

"Don't blame him. I insisted on coming. Thomas Jefferson is coming here. I received a message. With him will arrive justice for my husband, I am sure," said Jane.

Ruthanne spoke. "I need to see to the kitchen to make sure there are ample supplies."

"My dear," said Jane, "what an honor. You will have Mr. Jefferson at your wedding."

Ruthanne went into the kitchen as Fabric, Emilia, and the Catholic priest came out and were told the news.

"Anything I can do to help?" asked Father McKinsy.

"Is there a way we can arrange some seating here?" asked Major Plate, getting practical.

"That certainly makes up for not having it at the church," said Reverend Falldrem.

"A most eclectic mix of guests, but Mr. Jefferson is a man of the people. He won't mind," said Jane, looking almost happy.

"I happen to have some wine with me. If there is no objection since I understand Mr. Jefferson does partake?" said the priest.

"No. Absolutely no objection. Unless anyone else here objects?" No one did.

Genevieve returned, having dressed in record time.

The priest went out to get the wine from his saddlebags. Ruthanne returned from the kitchen.

"There's plenty of food," she said, with a look at Emilia. Emilia nodded and went back in the kitchen. Fabric followed.

Jane Penberthy fussed a little bit over Ruthanne's veil. "How lovely you look," she said with a crack in her voice.

Ruthanne appeared nervous.

"Thomas Jefferson. Who would have ever thought? An opportunity to meet him," Jane said encouragingly.

Said Genevieve, "the moment you've waited for all your life and one of the most important men in the country is going to be here."

"The most important moment of my life," Ruthanne said softly.

In her black mourning dress, Jane lost her original expression of surprise and now could not help but weep a little bit.

Reverend Falldrem embraced her.

Having seen to the food preparations, Ruthanne located her bag and rearranged the pillows on the couch.

"I am ready," she said to no one in particular.

"At last, a happy moment in all of this violence and grief," said Lantern, not feeling happy at all.

The celebratory nature of the event was contagious, if not joyous.

Emilia, Fabric, and Father McKinsy were busy in the kitchen.

Jane Penberthy indicated she wanted the company of the Protestant minister in a quiet corner of the room.

"I think there should be a little distance between the bride and groom," said Genevieve.

She directed Major Plate to stand near the front door and told Lantern to sit on a small chair behind him.

From that chair, Lantern could see out a small window.

Private Crier was posted outside in anticipation of greeting the carriage and opening the doors for the esteemed visitor.

"It's your job, Lantern, to keep the groom company if he starts getting fidgety. Calm him down with your practical conversation. And also alert us the minute you see a carriage coming through the fort gates. I'm going to sit with the bride," said Genevieve.

When Genevieve started to sit on the couch, Ruthanne stood up and walked to the other side of the front door.

"I suppose we can just stand in the corner. We will be the first to greet him," said Genevieve, following. She ignored the look Ruthanne gave that indicated she wanted to be alone.

Genevieve did allow Ruthanne to stand slightly in front.

After all, Ruthanne was the bride.

A quiet calm settled over the room. Lantern did not need to worry about the groom becoming tense. He was the epitome of calm, standing in an almost slothful manner.

In the quiet stillness, they could only hear the tick tock of the mantle clock and the snow come down.

"They're here!"

Lantern's excited voice came the same time as the sound of the coach pulling up near the front door reached the waiting party.

Outside, Private Crier opened the carriage door.

General Leshoward was in his full dress uniform with powdered wig as he stepped out of the carriage and extended his hand to the tall gentleman in similar dress, though formal civilian, not military.

All hearts were beating excitedly as the two men passed Private Crier and made their way to the front door of the house.

No one moved inside the house except Jane Penberthy.

She was halfway across the room when the door opened wide, temporarily covering both Major Plate and Lantern.

Looking like she wanted to greet the statesmen with open arms.

The honored guest crossed the threshold before the general.

"Mr. Jefferson!"

Jane Penberthy fairly screamed the name causing everyone to look in her direction instinctively

Even the woman who had the kitchen knife in her hand glanced at the widow in black.

Abruptly Ruthanne Webber pulled her elbow back, intending to thrust the knife upward into the breast of the man in front of her.

Before she had a chance, he had pulled his sword and thrust it deep into her heart.

Dead instantly, she fell to the floor, blood running all over the wedding dress, veil, and white cape.

Jane Penberthy laughed.

"What's going on?" cried Reverend Falldrem.

At the same time Major Plate relaxed his arm that had been holding Lantern still behind the door.

General Leshoward took hold of Jane Penberthy. Private Crier came up behind the swordsman.

"Well done," said Genevieve proudly.

Hayward Manchester, still holding his sword in one hand, reached up with the other and pulled off the white powdered wig.

"Damned uncomfortable," he said, looking at the limp hair.

He set the sword down beside the dead woman and dropped the wig on top of it.

Chapter 45

As Genevieve and Lantern watched, Private Crier supervised the removal of Ruthanne's body, appearing proud of the small role he had played in the entrapment.

Reverend Falldrem had taken Jane Penberthy home.

Father McKinsy was still with Fabric and Emilia in the kitchen.

General Leshoward was shedding his dress uniform in his room.

The two other men had gone over to the soldier's barracks to change clothes.

Genevieve pulled an envelope from her robe.

Father McKinsy emerged, and said goodbye. The general followed the priest outside and spent some time conferring with him.

Inside, Genevieve took the envelope into the food preparation area. Lantern followed her.

Fabric and Emilia were interrupted in the middle of an embrace.

"These are your freedom papers, Fabric. I added a 'k' to your name and made it a surname. I chose the Christian name of Steven."

Lantern was surprised. "But I thought I had the papers."

"Hush, Lantern. These are the papers I have prepared for you, Fabric. And also, there is a marriage license. Totally fictitious preacher, I am afraid, but that was the best I could do."

"That's okay. We were just married by Father McKinsy. We have a paper," said Emilia, holding up a half page.

"I'd burn that one. It could be traced to him and someone might ask questions. But it's up to you," Genevieve said.

"Best you go now," said Shears Plate from the doorway. He was now dressed in more casual clothing than Lantern had ever seen him wear. "I've got two good horses from the Melton estate. They will never be missed."

"Right and there's a bill of sale for the horses, too. I just wanted to go over the names with you, Emilia. I gave you the maiden name Sanchez-White. Is that all right?" Genevieve asked.

"That will do fine," said Emilia.

"We will be forever grateful. To all of you. Especially you, Mistress Genevieve," said Fabric.

"It will be a long hard life, if you are caught. Even if you are not," Plate said.

"We want to go somewhere where there's no chance that slavery will follow," said Emilia.

"Just because you are not a slave doesn't mean you will be treated as an equal," Lantern said.

"We understand. I am prepared to claim that I have African blood in my ancestry," said Emilia.

"But that is not true?" Genevieve asked.

"No, Mistress. It is not true. But this will be the last time I ever admit that to any human being. How can anyone ever prove what is truly in the blood?"

"And that lie will not go against your creed?" Lantern asked.

"I think God will understand and forgive me."

"Godspeed to the two of you, I've also here a notation that you served your country, Fabric, by helping us expose a traitor. It's just a handwritten note signed by General Leshoward," said Plate.

"When did he have a chance to sign that?" asked Lantern.

"Lantern, don't you think I can do my uncle's signature in my sleep? Knowing he was immersed in this little colony, obsessed with the widows bereaved by his famous victory, out of touch with the national government, I have done much good work in his name over the years. So long as he doesn't deny it if somebody questions it."

"He won't," said Lantern. "I will see to that."

"Good," said Genevieve. "Now agents from Philadelphia are bound to be on their way. Fortunately, our ruse worked and we flushed Ruthanne out in the open. But we still don't have everyone."

Hayward Manchester entered. For a few seconds he and Fabric stood side by side.

Lantern was struck by how similar they looked.

Both muscular, tall, with bronzed skin and high cheekbones, healthy with long arms and legs and closely cut hair.

Then swiftly Fabric and Emilia took their papers and small bags with their personal belongings out to the horses Major Plate had procured.

They rode off silently into the snow.

Chapter 46

"Is Abigail Fichton safe?" Genevieve asked her uncle when he came back in.

"Yes," he replied, without adding any detail.

"She was my contact here. We were together during the war. Soldier's wives following their husband's campaigns. When I began my work for the government, I was given her name as a safe person to call upon if I were ever in the same vicinity. Apparently she is under some kind of special protection?" Genevieve asked.

"Yes," said Leshoward, again without elaborating.

"I like to never have found her. In fact, she first communicated with me through Emilia."

"She is in a safer place. Too many people are looking for her."

"Ruthanne was looking for her," said Major Plate.

"I knew she did not know who to trust. But my biggest problem was I knew I could never convince you, Uncle, that I was a government agent, much less that these women were a dangerous group. I knew you would not trust me," Genevieve said.

"I truly believed they were war widows trying to better themselves," Leshoward said.

"He was not the only one who believed that," said Lantern loyally.

"The vast majority were. A small percentage were witches, believers of the dark arts. They were mere pawns in the larger game. But while we suspected there were political agents infiltrating this group, my original assignment concerned Reginald Penberthy," said Genevieve.

"What was Thistle Mannstein's connection?" asked Lantern.

"There are two groups attempting to instill terror in Europe and America. One is the anarchist group I have been tracking. The other we know little about. A maverick element of terror stealthily moving within society under the guise of being monarchists but are actually darker in nature. We believe a liaison between those two groups was in this area," said Genevieve. "And we now know that person was Thistle Mannstein, an anarchist tied to European assassins."

"And they sent her to Kentucky?" asked Lantern.

"Kentucky is important," said Hayward.

"We heard rumors there was an assassination attempt planned in Kentucky. News of the gala reached Philadelphia about the same time but no one made a connection," said Genevieve.

"The gala provided a structure for Thistle Mannstein to do her job- weaken our governmental system by means of terror. Add fear of death to the cost of serving in a democracy and you drastically reduce the number of people willing to do so," said Major Plate.

"Who was Thistle, really?" asked Lantern.

"We are not sure. Certainly not an orphaned widow of the revolution," said Genevieve.

"She was not a monarchist?" asked Lantern.

"Far from it. Penberthy was the monarchist," Leshoward said.

"Yet, he was not Catholic," Lantern said.

"No, you don't have to be a Catholic to be a monarchist. He wanted us to return to England, not create our own monarchy," said Major Plate.

"Spies are not necessarily truthful about their religion. Penberthy was no Lutheran. Thistle was no Catholic. We know all about Penberthy. We may not know everything about Thistle, but we know what she intended," said Genevieve.

"Henri Mannstein had turned over all letters and papers found in his wife's personal desk to General Leshoward. Thistle had kept detailed records," noted Hayward.

"Yet we don't know who the other killers are," said the general.

Chapter 47

"We know from Thistle's papers that she was the Mistress Superior, having created the Weaving Mistresses for her own purposes. She was in contact with agents from Europe in connection with the assassination conspiracies which were uniting the subversive groups," said Genevieve. "She knew one member of the maverick group was already in her organization. But Thistle failed to find out that agent's identity."

"Likewise the agent was kept in the dark as to who Thistle was. We think the maverick agent was Hortense. Ignorant of one another's identities, another person's arrival was necessary for them to connect and the plan to proceed. This connection, we now know, was Ruthanne Webber," said Major Plate.

"Ruthanne was trusted by both groups," said the general.

"Yes, Hortense had the names of the assassins but was instructed to only reveal that information to Ruthanne. Ruthanne knew Thistle was the plan's organizer," said Genevieve.

"What?" Lantern expressed her confusion.

"It was like this. Thistle knew the assassination plan. She had a list of costumes to assign to certain guests. She did not know which of her Weaving Mistresses were the assassins," said Genevieve.

"Hortense had that information," said Major Plate.

"But Hortense disappeared," said Lantern.

"Right. Before she could complete the circle of information. But pooling their knowledge, Thistle and Ruthanne now knew who was marked to die and in which costume. Hayward Manchester in the costume of King Gustav," said Major Plate.

"The character was sort of a code for the victim?" Lantern asked. "Who was the intended victim? Hayward?"

"It must have been Hayward," said Genevieve. "We don't know why. My theory is he is of French royal descent."

Everyone looked at her.

"Perhaps not legitimately," Genevieve continued.

Everyone looked at Hayward. He shrugged.

"Regardless. Hayward, originally to be King Gustav, demanded to be Julius Caesar instead. Reginald Penberthy took the character of King Gustav," said Major Plate.

"So Thistle and Ruthanne had a dilemma. Two unknown women in the cult were going to kill whoever played the character of Gustav. But they knew the wrong person was going to be in that costume," said Genevieve.

"Thistle and Ruthanne decided to kill Hayward Manchester themselves. And just let events concerning whoever was going to kill Penberthy take their own course," Leshoward said.

"Isn't is important we find out why Hayward was the intended victim?" asked Lantern.

"No," said Genevieve.

"Yes," said Hayward.

"Meanwhile, one of the original assassins had lost her partner. Let's assume Prudence Horaceton and Hortense, herself, were the original assassins. Prudence was afraid to go it alone so she stages her own disappearance while also recruiting a newcomer to the cause," said Major Plate.

"We are getting into speculation here," said the general.

"Thistle's records clearly indicate two assassins. They could not have pulled it off with only one," said Genevieve.

"I find the misidentification of Prudence Horaceton as dead to be extremely implicating," said Major Plate. "If you ask me, Neilman Horaceton should be put under arrest. Perhaps his wife as well."

"I have soldiers watching the Horaceton house," said the general. "They are under orders to stop them if they attempt to leave."

"They won't try that," said Major Plate.

"Don't be too sure," said Genevieve. "They may think they have gotten away with this."

"I have to go soon to the Penberthy house to call on Jane, then run another errand," said the general. "I could pay the Horacetons a visit at the same time."

"We still have killers loose," said Major Plate. "I don't think Lantern and Genevieve should be left alone."

"I was figuring you and Hayward would be taking care of them," said Leshoward. "But I can postpone my errand for a time."

"I also see Prudence as probably one of the assassins," said Hayward.

"It all points to her," said Lantern.

"We cannot accuse her without evidence," said Leshoward.

"If Prudence Horaceton was the third assassin, then who was the fourth?" asked Lantern.

"Hortense Melton. Has to be. She showed up at the ball and then vanished," said Hayward.

"How do we know that?" Lantern asked.

"You saw her," said Major Plate. "Remember? You saw her remove her mask for an instant. I told you who she was based on her her having been previously announced."

"Yes, I remember. You told me to draw her," Lantern said.

"Did you?" Genevieve asked.

"Yes."

"Why don't you get the drawing, Lantern?" asked her father.

"No one ever asked me about that drawing again," she said. "Shears asked me to do these drawings, and the next thing I knew, he was marrying Ruthanne."

"That was an elaborately staged trap, with all of us playing scripted parts," said Hayward Manchester. "The idea actually originated with Mrs. Penberthy. She believed Ruthanne's behavior at the gala after the killings indicated guilt. She wants her husband's assassins punished."

"She consulted me privately," said the general.

"I was not informed," said Lantern.

She left the room briefly.

"I told you it was a mistake not to let her in on it from the beginning," said Hayward to Plate. "You will pay for it the rest of your life."

"It wasn't my decision," protested Major Plate.

"I take full responsibility," said the general.

"Nevertheless YOU will pay for it," said Hayward to Plate.

"She is so young," said Leshoward, somewhat sadly.

"I told you how I valued Lantern's consultations. And her talent for drawing faces," said Plate to Leshoward.

168

"I should have listened to you," said Leshoward.

Lantern returned with her art. Talk returned to the killings.

"This is the women I glimpsed," said Lantern.

"Lantern!" Major Plate picked up a detailed drawing of a fair woman in an ancient world costume.

"That is Hortense Melton. From when I saw her at the ball," said Lantern.

Major Plate pulled out a miniature from his coat.

"That is Hortense Melton. Ruthanne gave me this portrait of her when she reported her missing."

The two women, while both appearing fair and petite in the drawings, looked nothing alike in facial structure.

"Then who is this? Who did I draw?" asked Lantern.

Everyone else in the room already knew the answer.

"This is Prudence Horaceton," said Major Plate. "It only makes sense if Prudence Horaceton was posing as Hortense Melton at the ball. Hortense was never there."

"Then Hortense Melton must be the body found in the grave," said Hayward.

"Major Plate, you were right," said Leshoward. "They did find a replacement killer. But who?"

Chapter 48

Prudence was arrested the next day along with her husband.

"Prudence has denied everything," Leshoward reported.

Genevieve, Lantern, Major Plate, General Leshoward, along with Hayward, were once again at the Leshoward home trying to discern the identity of a female killer.

Prudence Horaceton would not talk.

But her male accomplice, at first unwitting, then a willing partner, had confessed.

"Neilman Horaceton says Prudence decided on her own to disappear when Hortense Melton was killed. She already had a supply trip planned and she simply went into hiding," Leshoward said.

"Yes, we know Hortense Melton was the corpse," Plate said.

"Who killed her?" Genevieve asked.

"We still don't know. We may never," said the general.

"The way I see it, when Hortense was killed, it threw them into a panic. They found her body and buried it in a shallow grave," said Major Plate.

"Ruthanne and Thistle hoped we would think Thistle was the dead body if that victim was found," said Leshoward.

"But Thistle had disappeared too late to be the dead woman. Too many people had seen her after the body was found," said Major Plate.

"Hayward had seen her at the party after Hortense had been killed," said Genevieve.

"Except I did not know the significance of the timing," said Hayward.

"Maybe that is when you became a designated victim," said Plate. "Maybe Penberthy was the original intended victim all along and you were added after that evening."

"That would make sense," said Leshoward.

"Yes," said Genevieve. "They could not have known Prudence would leave home."

"Prudence, on the other hand, had left home at just the right time," said Leshoward.

"When Prudence came to Thistle claiming she wanted to hide from her husband, Thistle had no idea she was an assassin. But she saw that another missing woman would be very convenient at that time," said Major Plate.

"Ruthanne hid both Thistle and Prudence easily at the Melton Farm. The elderly couple had set out for Philadelphia to search for their daughter. Slaves were not going to ask questions," said Genevieve. "Then Ruthanne lied, saying the body was not Hortense."

"Thistle decided to have Neilman identify Prudence as the dead woman. Prudence must have thought that was a wonderful idea. She could hardly be accused of assassination if she were dead," said Plate.

"Why did Horaceton agree to do that? And how did you find out he had lied?" Lantern asked.

"Originally, Horaceton was not in on this conspiracy. Neilman received a message from Prudence delivered innocently via their newest recruit Margaret Craig, and that was the beginning of his complicity. The body had been buried of necessity. He had only to lie about the clothing," Leshoward said.

"It was imperative the message reach him before he identified the clothing as not being his wife's," said Major Plate.

"We found Horaceton's letter at his home. A vital piece of evidence. It is very persuasive prose, convincing him Prudence was working in the service of her country. Delivery by a congressman's wife made it even more convincing," Leshoward said.

"Yes. Having him believe she was really missing was a great ploy. To his relief, he was presented evidence she was alive and she was calling upon him to join her in a passionate cause. The letter claimed she needed to appear to be dead for the sake of her own safety. He must identify the clothing as belonging to Prudence," said Plate.

"So he has little information that will help with the capture of the other assassin," mused Genevieve. "Prudence is holding out the identity of the fourth woman as her only card left in bargaining for her life."

"Right. We suspect only Prudence Horaceton knows the true identity of her accomplice."

Said Lantern, "I have more questions. Mainly about Ruthanne Webber. Who exactly was she and how did she get involved?"

"I tried to keep up with all of the widows of my men," said the general. "I had no idea she had become entangled with anarchists."

"Until I traveled with her, no one had any idea she was involved. Apparently, she had been recruited in Philadelphia. Isolated, well off, living alone, she was a good target. It was the general's matchmaking ideas that gave her a perfect excuse to travel to Kentucky and take part in the assassination," said Genevieve.

"My matchmaking has never come to any good," said Leshoward.

"That is so true," said Lantern.

"It was such a coincidence we were on the same trail ride. The only two women traveling alone, naturally we joined forces. She knew about the ball, knew about the attack on the king in Sweden. Knew all about the situation in France. I became suspicious. So I mentioned having heard a rumor that Thomas Jefferson was coming," said Genevieve.

"She reacted?" asked Hayward.

"She totally gave herself away with the expression on her face. I knew the conspiracy rumors must be true. Now I had a dilemma, I was to tell no one but how could I alone prevent an assassination?" said Genevieve.

"And I suppose Thomas Jefferson was never coming?" Lantern asked.

"Of course not," said Genevieve.

"More likely to see Fabric there," said Hayward.

"How did Emilia get involved with them?" asked Lantern.

"Emilia was recruited by Naomi, Thistle's maide. Convinced they were really all witches, Emilia, being a devout Catholic, went at once to her priest to betray them," said Genevieve.

"But he was conflicted about confessions of other of his flock. He was afraid religious prejudice would cause trouble. He convinced her to keep quiet, stay in the group, and just observe. But ultimately she told Fabric and he came to me," said Major Plate.

"Fabric told Emilia to take the same action Father McKinsy

directed, but to report to Major Plate instead," said Leshoward.

"The important information she gave us was that Ruthanne Webber was a secret member. By this time, I was betrothed to her. She made sure of that by having me at the Melton house with no chaperon," said Major Plate.

"How did you not suspect Ruthanne, being so close to her?" asked Genevieve.

"Genevieve!" protested Lantern.

"She is correct. But in my defense if you had been a little less deceptive about your position in all this, you might have made a difference, Madam," said the major to Genevieve.

"I felt there was something wrong from the beginning with your showing up here," Lantern declared. "Such a coincidence you came just in time for the ball."

"Have you told your cousin that you got her the character of Deborah Franklin?" Major Plate asked Genevieve with a smile.

"Is that really true?" Lantern asked.

Genevieve became defensive.

"You wanted a character so badly. When I manipulated the list, I added that detail for my own amusement."

"So you did not know the lists were involved in an assassination plot?" Lantern frowned.

"At first, I only thought to expose traitors," said Genevieve. "I still had no proof the gala was connected. I was following orders to prevent trouble."

"How was that supposed to happen?" Lantern asked.

"It was a plan from high up in the new government. A sort of revenge, but at the same time a means of preventing future trouble. It backfired, of course," said Genevieve. "I had a false list to plant to confuse the situation and expose Reginald Penberthy if he proved to still be loyal to England. After my trip with Ruthanne and other indications of a fatal plot, I had to think for myself."

"So what did you do?"

"I invented another list. The character Caesar was the most likely candidate for an assailant. I assumed he would be the target until I realized Gustav was shot at midnight on March 16. Of course

Caesar was killed on March 15. Allowing for a minor date discrepancy, our gala was in the wrong month- the middle of May, not the middle of March. I thought that did not matter. I read too much into symbolic historical significance and what was happening overseas, not paying enough attention to our own circumstances."

"Did you try to contact Philadelphia?" asked Leshoward.

"I did not dare trust anyone I did not know intimately. I warned Hayward to carry a weapon."

"I always do that anyway."

"Is the government that fragile?" asked Major Plate.

"I believe so," said Genevieve. "The educated powers on the east coast believe only their iron hand over the people will enable the country to survive. The ordinary person does not have the wits to fulfill the democratic potential."

"I disagree," said Major Plate. "We are not so gullible as they assume. And I did suspect Ruthanne. I was just not sure what was going on enough to act on my feelings. I thought it would all come out in the end."

"When did you suspect Ruthanne then?" Genevieve asked.

"From the beginning," said Major Plate.

"Really, from the beginning? Why?" asked Lantern.

"When she came into my office to report Hortense Melton missing, she was so false. Like a stage actress. She struck me that way from the first," said Major Plate.

"You said nothing," said Genevieve.

"Later, though, I put her attitude down to her knowing of our potential union and my being ignorant of it," said Major Plate.

"You might have told me of your suspicions instead of just saying you treasured my friendship and hoped it could endure. If any of you had trusted me, I might have put it all together," said Lantern.

"True. But by then he was under orders, Lantern. More important orders to court her," Leshoward said.

"I felt I had no choice but to carry on with the courtship and take her to the ball and see what happened," said Major Plate.

"So she arrived with you, in a red cloak, with her Weaving Mistress robe in a bag, and changed into her assassin's clothes right there under everyone's nose," Lantern said.

"And when it was over, Ruthanne only had to reappear in her red cloak. The discarded Helen costume was hers," Leshoward said.

"She ran when I killed Thistle. So she was out to redeem herself for that act of cowardice by sacrificing her life to kill Thomas Jefferson," said Hayward.

"It is ironic the only politician they killed was Penberthy," said the general.

"Why?" asked Lantern.

"The real danger to Leverageton was putting Reginald Penberthy in a position of power. Penberthy was a clandestine loyalist during the war," said her father.

"So was he involved in the conspiracy?" Lantern asked.

"I would prefer Jane Penberthy never know about her husband," said the general.

"There is no reason for it to ever be known," said Genevieve. "In the interest of our nation's security it is probably best if the lists never see the light of day."

"Surely it must come out if he was in on the assassination?" Lantern asked.

"We highly doubt that. He was an honorable man, if a traitor. He would not have condoned assassination," said the general.

"I believe that it should not come out. He is dead. It no longer matters," Hayward said.

"It all seems so random. The dead, I mean. They range from wealthy to servant. Who killed Naomi? And why?" Lantern asked.

"There was nothing random about this. Naomi had lied about Mrs. Fichton seeking refuge at the Mannstein home," Leshoward said.

"We don't know about Naomi. Prudence won't say or may not know. It could have been the fourth woman. Newly converted," said Major Plate.

"Practicing?" Genevieve asked.

"Possibly. She may never have killed before and did not want to risk reacting faintly at the crucial kill," Leshoward said. "Killing is not easy. It takes getting used to."

"Naomi had been killed the day of the ball. Very risky. Speaks of the new initiate or the unbalanced," said Major Plate.

"They overestimated what they could accomplish in a very short space and in a very short period of time," Leshoward said.

"Once identities were revealed there was little time to confer. They must have suddenly understood their stifled communication system had worked against them. What had begun as a simple plan had become too complicated as a result of too much secrecy," said Genevieve. "Assassinations are hard to plan."

They all looked at her.

"So I am told," said Genevieve nonchalantly.

"And to prevent," said Major Plate.

"I was taken unawares at the ball," Genevieve admitted. "They were very good at their deliberate distractions."

"Which were?" asked Lantern.

"First- Thistle Mannstein appeared magically and then disappeared. She cloaked her Helen of Troy costume with a robe and veil to accomplish this," said Major Plate.

"Meanwhile, Prudence has arrived in the decoy Helen of Troy costume," Leshoward said.

"There was a third Helen of Troy?" Lantern asked.

"Yes, Ruthanne. She kept her Helen costume covered by her red cloak, until the assassination," said Major Plate.

"So the fourth assassin did not have a Helen of Troy costume?" Genevieve asked.

"Or escaped in it," Lantern speculated.

"Let's get back to what we do know," Leshoward said.

"Adapting quickly, Prudence convinced Horaceton not to say anything. And Thistle and Ruthanne not to kill him," said Major Plate.

"They told Horaceton he was a hero and it would soon be over. Just wait patiently for Prudence to come to him. He was thrilled. Surrounded for years by all these war heroes and now it would be his turn," Leshoward said.

"And after?" Lantern asked.

"She would be right back in ordinary clothes and they would be on their way," Leshoward said.

"So what went wrong?" Lantern asked.

"Henri Mannstein had seen his wife. He had been clinging to Naomi's ethereal prediction that Thistle would appear at the ball as Helen of Troy. So he was looking for her to be Helen of Troy. And there she was! Ecstatic that she was alive, he was rushing to her side," Leshoward said.

"He followed her and caught up to her for a few seconds. Thistle sent him after me. If he had not gone, he surely would have been killed right then. I was preoccupied with trying to find her during the killings," said Major Plate somewhat sadly. "Like a magic trick, Thistle had reappeared as Helen. Then vanished just as promptly. While Mannstein and I were on this wild goose chase, Thistle had put on her concealing costume."

"As did Ruthanne. They turned Mannstein's unexpected interference into the perfect diversion," Leshoward said.

"Where were you, Father?" Lantern asked.

"I had stepped out. Someone wanted to talk to me at that moment."

"Remember, like me, he knew nothing about the violence," said Genevieve. "I think we were both deliberately distracted."

"Not in my case. I was with Abigail Fichton," the general said.

"Penberthy and I were announced within minutes of each other," recalled Hayward.

"Prudence and her partner attacked Penberthy and killed him. Ruthanne and Thistle attacked Hayward with a much different result," Major Plate continued.

"Where did the assassins go then?" asked Lantern.

"Prudence had her costume under her robe all the time, so she simply sheds her robe," Leshoward said.

"Thistle is dead. Ruthanne runs and puts her red cloak back on. Blood won't show on the cloak," said Genevieve.

"Ruthanne gets cleanly away. She slips right back into the group. No evidence she is involved. But I confided my suspicions to Jane. She convinced the general. Thus our trap for her at the 'wedding' with our fantasy guest," said Major Plate.

"She had shown cowardice the first time. She was too fanatical to let that happen again. And she would have willingly sacrificed her life to kill Thomas Jefferson," Leshoward said.

"She probably thought I was too minor a target to die for," said Hayward.

"Getting back to the gala, Prudence and her confederate ran also. The accomplice must have slipped back into the crowd successfully," said Major Plate.

"But Prudence slips up. Exactly how we do not know yet. The impromptu secondary goal is accomplished. Penberthy dies. The main mission has failed. Manchester lives. Thistle dies instead. Yet two killers successfully get away. But for Prudence, something goes wrong. The result is Margaret Craig is mortally wounded, Emilia is injured, and Prudence, herself, has a flesh wound. Still, for a short time she manages to turn the episode into the appearance of an attack on herself," Leshoward said.

"Prudence was able to claim that the blood on her clothing was from her encounter with Emilia. She still denies that she had anything to do with Margaret Craig's injury," said Major Plate.

"It makes no sense for Margaret Craig's attacker to have been Ruthanne. She would not have had time. She had to drop the robe, move away from it and retrieve her red cloak. Thistle was dead instantly so Margaret's attacker was either Prudence or the unknown fourth woman," said the general.

"Do they know who that is yet?" Lantern asked.

"They think it may be me," said Genevieve.

"Nobody believes that," said Lantern loyally.

"The evidence against you was planted," said Leshoward. "We know that now."

"I'm still suspected by others. I still do not dare leave the fort. Not until the fourth killer is exposed," said Genevieve.

Chapter 49

"I need the papers you kept for me," said Genevieve to Lantern when the subject of the murders seemed to be exhausted temporarily.

"So what are these papers that you gave me to keep for you?" Lantern asked.

"You have not opened to them?" Genevieve asked.

"You told me they were the papers for Emilia and Fabric. Obviously, that was not true. Are they for a different set of people?"

"No, they are about people. Many people. They are lists of spies. Spies from the war nearing 20 years ago. Loyalist spies and patriot spies. The anarchists were not the only ones planning to use this masquerade ball. Our government was also going to use it. But to expose people, not assassinate them. The character assignations were the key to identifying traitors," said Genevieve.

"You are telling me all this has to do with who was what character at the masquerade ball?" Lantern asked.

"Yes. Before we knew anything about assassinations, certain people in Philadelphia decided it would be a good idea to let some of the people here in Kentucky know where everyone had stood during the Revolutionary War. So we devised a simple plan. A list of characters was drawn up and the assignation of those characters was an accusation of treachery on one side or the other," said Genevieve.

"There is such a list?" asked the general.

"It sprang from old feelings that run deep. It is a list of those who were traitors and never found out. They had been given certain characters to portray at the ball as a means of identifying them," said Genevieve.

"And what will happen when these identifications are made?" Major Plate asked.

"The loyalists will be disgraced. Certainly banned from the colony. Some of them may be charged with crimes or jailed or exiled. I don't know all the legal details. The patriots will probably be applauded if they are still in the colonies. If they fled to England with their families they may have to face consequences there," said Genevieve.

"This war has been over for years. We are no longer colonies. We are states. Kentucky will become a state next month. How do you think dredging up all of these old differences is going to help? People will die if these lists come out," said Major Plate.

"The list has been tampered with and it's all now a mess," said Genevieve.

"So what is supposed to happen now?" Lantern asked.

"We are having such a cold spring. It is getting a little chilly in here. I think we should have a fire lit in the fireplace. Does anyone object?" Genevieve asked.

"I do not," said Leshoward.

Major Plate and Lantern met one another's eyes.

"I can speak for both of us," said Major Plate. "We do not object."

"Does he speak for both of you?" asked Genevieve, somewhat aggravated.

"He speaks for both of us," Lantern said.

As the fire came to life and hungrily ate up the pages of the lists, Genevieve muttered to herself. "No man will ever speak for me."

Hayward remained diplomatically silent.

The general brought forth an envelope. It contained the list sent to him from Philadelphia before the gala.

He tossed it into the flames.

Chapter 50

News came from the east the next day.

"The Meltons were found dead in Philadelphia. Viciously attacked and robbed in their fine carriage. But no one knows what happened. An estate agent is liquidating their property for a distant cousin in Canada," reported Major Plate.

He was now formally the recipient of all official correspondence.

The news, after all that had happened, made little impact.

The second part of the message was more disheartening.

Officials from Philadelphia were on their way to officiate at Prudence's trial.

They still had no idea who the missing killer was.

"So what will happen to Prudence?" Lantern asked.

"She'll be hanged," Leshoward said. "I may not fare much better."

"I don't see how they can possibly blame you. If they hang Prudence we will never know who her accomplice was in killing Reginald Penberthy," Hayward said.

He was spending more time at the fort than at home these days. His courtship of Genevieve was now completely open.

"The fourth attacker has still not been identified," Leshoward said. "A congressman's wife died. They will see that as my responsibility."

"Poor Margaret Craig. She suffered so badly," Lantern said.

"I will never forget how she lay on that clean floor in the butler's pantry," Hayward said. "I glimpsed her that night when you sent me to talk to Craig. But I only looked in and did not enter the room. It was a scene I will never forget. So barren."

Lantern froze.

"What was her costume under her cloak?"

"She, um, wasn't wearing one," said the general. "Don't you recall she was wearing undergarments? Poor woman."

"Yes." Lantern frowned as if deep in thought.

"Genevieve, I have some ideas to talk over with you privately.

General, may I take your niece for a nighttime carriage ride? If the major will allow me to borrow his carriage?" Hayward asked.

"I need no one's permission, do I, Uncle?" Genevieve asked.

Major Plate responded in affirmative to the blacksmith at the same time the general responded similarly to his niece.

Hayward and Genevieve left.

"Shears, I want to talk to you about something urgent," Lantern said to Major Plate.

"Perhaps I'll just go for a ride myself," said the general.

"I think we can talk about our future now," said Major Plate.

"Never mind about our future. I think I know who the fourth assassin is now..."

Chapter 51

An impromptu meeting of the men in power in the colony was scheduled for the next evening at the tea parlor.

Reverend Falldrem would be there. Congressman Craig was coming. Also, Father McKinsy, Hayward Manchester, and Henri Mannstein were invited.

General Leshoward was gone again. Major Plate was to represent him.

Shears Plate and Marchmont Craig coincidentally met on the road to town and rode the rest of the way together.

The two men talked about Margaret Craig.

"I have not only lost my wife but also my unborn child, far too early in his or her life to have any chance to survive on its own."

There was a respectful silence for a short time. Only the sound of the horse's hooves on the road was audible.

The congressman asked why the general was not coming to the meeting.

"He's gone again."

"What does he do on those trips of his? A woman?"

"I've really no idea."

"I hear you are in line to become his son-in-law?"

"Possibly."

The men arrived at their destination only to find a note pinned to the door. The meeting had been called off, pending a promised complete confession the next day by Prudence Horaceton, naming the fourth assassin.

"Well, a wasted ride," said Craig.

"Not an unpleasant one, I hope, Congressman."

"No, certainly not. A nice clear night and you were good company. By the way, what of the witch, Prudence Horaceton? She is confined properly?"

"Indeed. She is shackled to a small bed in the empty cabin in the woods as the local jail has no capacity for females," said Major Plate.

"I fear the fourth accomplice will never be truly named," said the congressman.

"You could be right," said Major Plate. "But we think we will eventually get the real name from Prudence. She weakens every time a soldier interrogates her."

Plate laughed suggestively.

"They take pleasure from her?" Craig asked in surprise. "Leshoward allows that?"

"He is no longer completely in charge."

"Well, well. Tell me more."

Major Plate related how as each volunteer soldier, some volunteering more than once, had taken satisfaction from her over the past few days, she had been persuaded to reveal a little more of the details of the conspiracy.

"Come dark, we leave her alone. Too many coyotes to risk a guard being hurt," said Plate.

"Very wise," said Craig. "So she is talking?"

"She's holding out the name of the last assassin. The one that joined her in stabbing Penberthy. She fears being lynched if she is of no further value in providing information."

"What hope has she?"

"She had delusions of being rescued by confederates from the east."

"I see," said Craig thoughtfully.

"Can I accompany you back to your home or perhaps somewhere else? I will just go on out to the woods to intercept Hayward Manchester in case he has not left yet."

"No, go on and try to find Manchester. I have business at the fort. I want to talk with some of the soldiers about more security in the town and how it can better be administered. I want to get their perspective."

Marchmont Craig let Major Plate go his way and did not stir his horse until he thought the soldier was gone.

But Major Plate had only ridden a short distance away to see what the congressman would do.

Major Plate watched as Craig rode down the lane away from town.

He did not ride towards the fort.

184

Chapter 52

Two sentries stood outside the small cabin until it turned dark.

Prudence was bound to the bed inside as Major Plate had described to Congressman Craig.

The sentries bade her goodnight before leaving.

She cursed them openly, begging not to be left alone. They assured her they would fasten the door so no wild beast could enter.

She was half-asleep when she heard the door to the cabin creak open.

She was safe from animal, not man.

She screamed as he came near her. She felt the cold as her covers were ripped from her and a chill down her spine as a cold steel blade was pressed against her exposed flesh.

"You are going to suffer like she did," a voice rasped.

She screamed again, helpless, expecting pain.

"First, you are going to make it up to me some," said her visitor.

Suddenly, a light flared from the doorway.

Major Plate and Hayward Manchester rushed in the open door and grabbed the man's arms, pinning them back.

"I was just going to give her the same pain she gave Margaret," Marchmont Craig yelled as he struggled. "You cannot possibly blame me for wanting to kill her."

"Oh, but we do," said Major Plate, looking down at the congressman's open trousers. "I think you had a preliminary action in mind before you killed her didn't you?"

Hayward Manchester yanked the captive's pants up with one deft movement.

"She's an animal, no more than an animal. Look at what she did to my wife," the congressman cried.

Craig tried to jerk free.

Hayward punched him in the stomach.

"You're lucky that was my fist and not my sword," he said calmly to the collapsing man. He pulled a sheet over Prudence.

"Come on," said Major Plate, pulling Marchmont towards the door.

Hayward picked up his lantern.

"What about me?" yelled Prudence from the bed, as Plate and Hayward dragged Craig out of the cabin.

"Sleep well," Hayward called back at her.

Without any other action, he left the door to the cabin open.

A coyote howled.

Chapter 53

"I had to send Plate back to the cabin to shut the door so she wouldn't freeze to death or a wild animal get her," said Leshoward to his daughter, when she complained that Major Plate was not at the gathering before the fireplace in the Leshoward home.

"I'm afraid I'm the one who didn't shut the door," Manchester grinned.

"You should have had to ride back there," Lantern complained.

"Hey, he didn't have to say anything about it," said Hayward. "He's too self-disciplined."

"He is a soldier," said Leshoward. "And a gentleman."

"Appears you are neither," said Genevieve, winking at Hayward.

"I'm a soldier when it's time to fight, not in peace. I don't take orders well," said Hayward, smiling at Genevieve. "And I will never be a gentleman."

Major Plate entered, brushing the snow off his jacket.

"Prisoner secured."

"Get there before the coyote?" Hayward Manchester asked.

"Barely," said Plate.

"Damn," said Manchester.

"I had to shoot at it."

"That's a shame," said Manchester.

"Don't worry. I missed."

"That means the door might get left open tomorrow night."

"We do need a jail that accommodates both sexes," said Leshoward. "But that won't be my concern soon."

Before anyone could ask him what that meant, Reverend Falldrem knocked on the door.

He had visited the congressman in jail and had new information.

Marchmont Craig had confessed to the preacher.

"Prudence Horaceton recognized a vulnerable woman devoted to a husband whose very existence depended on his social position," said the reverend. "Margaret Craig was indeed the fourth assassin."

The minister knew even more details.

Prudence had trained Margaret to kill quickly.

"First, they practiced with the sheep, then with Naomi. Prudence told her husband about the plot then. Craig saw his future secured. So when he was told the plan, he simply did nothing to stop it."

"Marchmont is characteristically a follower, not a leader," said the general.

"He just didn't know his wife was going to be an active participant. Nor that the other assassins planned to kill her as well," said the minister.

"That may be true," said Leshoward.

"Why didn't Margaret tell him the whole plot?" Genevieve asked.

"Marchmont did not know the answer to that question," said Falldrem.

"She probably was afraid he would stop her. Undoubtedly, Prudence told her she was vital to the plan now that Hortense was dead. And she was," said Major Plate.

"I knew Margaret Craig had to be the fourth assassin because of the food," Lantern said.

"Yes, Lantern put it all together," said Major Plate.

"I don't understand," said Falldrem.

"She was attacked supposedly carrying a tray of food from the kitchen. Yet there was only the tray. No food scattered on the floor. It was clean. So clean. She was dying on a clean floor. Not even a broken dish," Lantern said.

"She had rushed to the pantry and grabbed an empty tray. That was her plan to blend back into the crowd," said Major Plate.

"It also occurred to me the costumes designated the killers just as they marked the victim," said Lantern.

"The costume that no longer fit Mrs. Craig was another version of Helen of Troy. We found it among her clothing," said Plate.

"They probably always planned to kill her. It was too risky to leave her to talk. She was too unstable. Plus with her dead, they had the congressmen under their thumb," Leshoward said. "They could then blackmail him. He would have to vote as they instructed or be disgraced by her actions."

"Poor foolish woman," said the minister.

Chapter 54

Father McKinsy arrived as Reverend Falldrem departed.

"Evil begets pain and suffering," commented Father McKinsy upon being told the latest news. "But Margaret Craig's suffering was no less real."

The priest and the general were planning to ride towards town together. Stepping outside also, Major Plate and Lantern were talking with them as they prepared their horses.

Genevieve and Hayward remained alone in the house.

"Why did she claim she killed Hayward Manchester instead of Reginald Penberthy? Was there a political target? Or did they not care who they killed, just so they disrupted the gala?" Lantern asked.

"Our only clue was the dying words of Margaret Craig. They would seem to support either side depending on how they are interpreted. She got confused in her mind the names Reginald Penberthy and Hayward Manchester, perhaps? Knowing the targets and realizing she had killed one, she became confused," Leshoward said.

"Or, in the chaos, she believed Thistle killed Hayward instead of the reverse. Then her guilt might have manifested itself in the statement that she killed Hayward instead, thinking that although she did not strike a blow at him, the intent was the same as the deed," Plate said.

"I think it was simpler. She knew Penberthy. Was friends with him and his wife. She killed a friend in disguise, realizing his identity too late. But Manchester was a stranger. Perhaps she could bear the burden of having killed a stranger and not her social equal," Leshoward speculated.

"And we don't think anybody told her that Manchester was still alive before she died?" asked the priest.

"Heavens, man. We had no idea she was one of the assassins. We thought she was an innocent victim," said Major Plate.

"Prudence now claims Ruthanne waylaid Margaret and deliberately killed her in cold blood because she feared Margaret would confess. Mrs. Craig was a new recruit, somewhat unsteady in her belief, motivated less by religion than by anger that her husband might be passed over by the power brokers," Leshoward said.

"And she was asked to step out of the choir," Lantern said.

"I don't know how strong of a motivating factor that was. Not making the choir does not cause most Christian women to turn to witchcraft and become assassins," the priest said.

"Since the clergy are all gentlemen, I think most underestimate the value ladies place on their contribution to worship," said Lantern.

The men smiled and nodded at this comment but she did not return their gestures.

At this point the general and the priest concluded their preparations and rode off, leaving Major Plate and Lantern still discussing the recent events and future plans.

"You don't agree with the priest?" Plate asked Lantern as they watched the two men ride away.

"It was more than she was not eligible for the choir. She had been in the choir and was asked to leave. When there were fewer people in the colony they were happy for her to sing in the choir, but then when more people joined they only wanted people who could sing better," Lantern said.

"Thinking along those lines, when there were fewer people in the colony and statehood seemed a long way away, everyone was happy with Marchmont Craig doing all of the political dirty work. But then when more people moved in they started looking at a more attractive personality," said Major Plate.

"And Marchmont Craig? Will he hang as a co-conspirator also?" Lantern asked.

"No, it's being hushed up with him. After all, he was caught in the act of attempting to ravage a prisoner. Have to let go of half of the guards in the land if we prosecuted that. And he swears he had no idea Margaret was involved in a murder plot. He figured it out after the fact just like we did," said Major Plate.

"Do you believe that?"

"No, but what can I do?" asked Major Plate.

"The new government wants it kept quiet," Lantern said.

"Corruption already at the highest levels," said Major Plate.

"Those two terms are synonymous- corruption and the highest levels," Lantern said.

"Anyway, he is being given a choice of some kind. I presume it will be exile. Maybe the Royalists will take him in and he will live in England."

"Maybe," Lantern said, wondering what England was like.

"And Henri Mannstein remains in Kentucky."

"So are you sure, that Henri Mannstein is totally innocent?" asked Lantern.

"Sure as can be. Ironically it was Mannstein who worried about witchcraft. That alone points to his innocence."

As Lantern and Major Plate talked about him, Congressman Marchmont Craig was many miles away on the trail to Philadelphia. He looked over his letter of resignation and properly made sure it was dried and sealed. He left it with one of his traveling companions and took off into the woods, saying he was going to shoot something fresh for dinner and wanted to make sure the document did not get lost or dirty.

He had the tickets to England in his pocket when he shot himself.

By the time news of his 'hunting accident' would reach back to Kentucky, most of those who knew his story would be gone.

Chapter 55

"So are we being told that our experiment in religious tolerance is coming to an end as soon as statehood is finalized?"

The next evening Major Plate and Lantern were having dinner at the Mannstein home with Genevieve, Hayward, Mrs. Penberthy, and Henri Mannstein.

The latter had asked the question.

"It looks like that could be the case. The Weaving Mistresses have to be disbanded because of the actions of a few," said Major Plate.

"Yes, that's been the case for ages," Hayward said.

"I thought our new democracy was going to change all of that," said Lantern.

"I don't think our experiment in tolerance will fail if you will remain within the community," said Major Plate to Mannstein.

"I debated going back east to the Catholic community there. I have not made a final decision. In the interim, I am thinking of sending for a woman from Europe to be my wife."

"I may not be here," said Lantern regretfully.

"We will. Hayward and I will marry and live at the fort. We are going to purchase the house. When might your bride arrive?" Genevieve asked.

"It will be months after I send for her. I'm wondering how she will be received?"

"I will welcome her," said Jane Penberthy. "I speak German. I will teach her English."

"You speak German, Mrs. Penberthy?" asked Mannstein with some surprise.

"My primary heritage." She smiled deeply at him.

"Perhaps I should not rush into sending for a bride so soon," Mannstein said.

Mrs. Penberthy smiled deeper.

"I should let some time pass away from this terrible event," said Henri Mannstein.

"There is one thing I was wondering? If it is not too painful to ask?" Major Plate asked.

"No. It is not painful like it was at first," said Mannstein, smiling again at Jane.

"How did Thistle get out of the room?" asked Major Plate.

"Simple. Naomi took her place in the game before she went in. When we opened the room and saw it empty, Naomi was actually there but she was so slight, she was behind the furniture. She appeared behind me while I was asking for the keys. We thought she had not been there until then," said Mannstein.

"I see," said Major Plate.

"Who killed Naomi?" asked Mannstein.

"It was Margaret Craig. She was practicing at the behest of Prudence Horaceton," said Major Plate. "Prudence was infuriated at the death of Hortense. Apparently they were secretly close. Partner assassins. She confessed she found out Naomi and Thistle buried Hortense after Ruthanne found her dead in the swing. Ruthanne told her how they mutilated Hortense so Prudence chose Naomi as Margaret's practice kill in retaliation."

"I suspect then Thistle marked Mrs. Craig for death at that moment. She loved Naomi so. If she had survived this tragedy, she certainly would have killed Mrs. Craig herself, and Mrs. Horaceton also, if she could have," said Mannstein.

"It is hard to believe you can live with someone and not really know them," said Jane sympathetically.

"That is so true," said Henri Mannstein solemnly.

All thinking of the truth about Jane's late husband, Genevieve and Hayward and Lantern and Major Plate looked at each other and wondered.

But they said nothing.

Chapter 56

"So the cabin where Fabric lived nearby is now officially abandoned?" Major Plate addressed General Leshoward.

Returning from his errand, the general had been informed of an official change in the status of his daughter's relationship with his second-in-command.

Having been told flatly by Lantern that she was going to marry Plate, he was attempting to have a somewhat more traditional conversation with his future son-in-law.

Just for the sake of propriety.

"Yes, that is the case."

"Then, General, I am officially requesting consent to occupy it."

"With my daughter?"

"Yes, General, that was to be my next request. Lantern's hand in marriage."

"You never have told me anything about your background. Don't you think as your prospective father-in-law I am entitled to know something?"

"There's very little to tell."

"Try me. I have made much out of little before," Leshoward said.

"My parents are farmers. They live in Virginia. They are good Presbyterians. I have written and kept them informed about the situation here. They are not thrilled that I have decided to settle here simply because it is so far away. We're counting on the new postal service to help us keep in touch. I have four sisters and two brothers. I am the second of the brothers. My four sisters were born first."

"Your parents had four girls and then three boys?"

"Yes, General," said Major Plate.

"All healthy? Your mother healthy?"

"Yes, General."

"They must believe in miracles."

"Yes, General. As a matter fact I think they do."

"No imbeciles or madness in the family?"

"No, General," said Major Plate.

"Criminals? Horse thieves? Charlatans?"

"None that I know, General," said Major Plate.

"I guess I don't have any choice but to consent. Now that the soldiers are being deployed further west, I think you're the only eligible young male left in Leverageton," Leshoward said.

"Think that might be an exaggeration, General. But I am deeply honored and grateful for your consent."

"Good. Since we're going to be relatives, although I'm a general, you're nothing but a major. I will put forth a situation to you that in perhaps different circumstances I might be asking, not for your consent mind you, but for your opinion, are rather perhaps your blessing."

"Yes, General?" asked Major Plate.

"I've been alone a long time. I'm proposing to take a second wife."

"Second wife? Uh- my congratulations, General. Is there anyone in particular? I mean, is it a settled issue? Mrs. Penberthy?" Major Plate could not help all his words coming out as questions as he processed this new situation.

"No indeed. It is a settled issue. Not to take from Lantern's event, we have already set our date for a fortnight away. And it is not Mrs. Penberthy."

"Oh, I'm sure Lantern is planning on the traditional nine-month engagement."

"That's what I suspected. Tradition is not that important to my fiancée," Leshoward said.

"Could I have some clue as to who this fortunate lady might be?" asked Major Plate.

"I thought you were the mystery solver, Major Plate."

"I've not detected this. Does Lantern know?" asked Major Plate.

"I think she has a hint. The lady is known to both of you. She has been staying at the convent and I have just returned from there. I brought her back with me and she is upstairs at my house right now."

"Who?"

"Mrs. Abigail Fichton."

Chapter 57

"I have a confession to make, Abigail," said General Leshoward, as he packed.

"Yes, Ronald?"

"I was the one that denounced you to your congregation as a possible witch."

"Go on." Abigail stood in the doorway of his bedroom.

"When you came to me that night at the camp with the plans for the battle I struggled with my conscience and then decided to take your advice and abandon my previous strategy. Then the battle went exactly as you planned. We won. We would've lost if I had used my strategy and we won on yours," Leshoward said.

"I always knew it was you."

"I told myself it was my Christian duty to bring your supernatural insight to the attention of the church where you worshiped. I told myself it was for the sake of your soul. I emphasized to them that I thought your ability was innocent, perhaps beyond your control, an evil influence," Leshoward said.

"You can only have thought my ability was an evil influence if you were on the side of the British."

"I did not realize that what I did would lead to your total ostracism from society. I tried to make up for it by making sure you had a place to live and that no one molested you. I allowed Fabric near you to keep an eye on you and provide his strength for when you needed a masculine hand," Leshoward said.

"That was a magnanimous gesture that endeared you to my heart. I knew you needed money here and you could've taken possession and sold him and solved your financial problems."

"Let's put all that aside. I've examined my decision to denounce you many times over the years. I came to the conclusion many years ago that, while not the deciding factors, that my wife was seriously ill and would soon die and that your husband perished in the battle that your clairvoyance helped us win, were important contributors to my decision," Leshoward said.

Abigail walked over to Leshoward and took his hand.

"I think I fell in love with you that night you came to me in the tent," he said simply.

"I want say that I fell in love with you that night," said Abigail. "My marriage was arranged. I did not know my husband well. But he was a good brave man. I do know that. In my mind, he was going to be the rock on which my future depended. Had he not been killed I most certainly would have based my entire life on serving him."

"Instead you have led a life of loneliness and misery that could be laid at my feet," said Leshoward.

"Not so. I have found happiness and contentment at my life. It is a great joy when the Lord allows me to relieve suffering through my herbal remedies. The rock on which I had planned to base my life crumbled before my eyes but it was replaced by a better stronger Rock. One that will never crumble."

"You never hated me?"

"I told you I'm not a witch. I'm a Christian. And sometimes-"

"Can we leave it at that? I experienced you coming to my camp warning me about the enemy's movements and predicting exactly what I should do to achieve victory. I concluded that your in-depth knowledge was beyond your capacity to ascertain in an earthly fashion and that events went as you predicted so closely that you had to have some type of supernatural knowledge of what the future had held," Leshoward said.

"What I would like to explain-"

"That's just it. Don't explain. That is all I can handle. I don't want to know anymore. I simply want you to stand by me the rest of your life or mine."

"Are you asking me to marry you?"

"Correct." Leshoward started to get down on one knee.

"That's not necessary. At your age, your knees must be going bad. I've but one question. Would I be allowed to continue my herbal medicines?"

"I will defend that right for you to the point of my death. And my knees are just fine, thank you."

"Then I accept. I will be your wife. My expertise will keep your knees in good shape."

"I think you should know that does not mean you will be mistress of the fort," he said smugly. "I received orders relieving me of command here. I have diplomatically decided to retire."

"Where will we be then?"

"My son has been tending my lands out west. I wrote to him some time ago. Actually that night after the murders at the masquerade ball I wrote to him that I would be coming soon to live on my property. It will not be an easy life. But I would be so happy if you would consider sharing it with me."

"I think I should be quite happy in such a place."

"You would be mistress of a plantation. Very small at first. I hope to grow it through horses rather than slaves. I am buying some of the Melton stock. But you would not be alone. My son has taken a wife. I got the news in his last letter."

"What about Lantern? Is she coming?"

"I don't know about Lantern yet. But there is plenty of room," Leshoward said.

"It sounds wonderful. When do we leave?"

"Within three days."

"Ronald, there is one more thing."

"Yes?"

"Part of our future will be built on blood that I spilt," said Abigail.

"What?"

"My premonition that I refused to tell you about. It concerned Reginald Penberthy. His life and death."

"I know. I gathered as much. You dropped enough hints that it was he in danger at the gala. I went to warn him. It did no good. He ignored me. I had no plausible explanation to give him for my concern. What could I say? The information was given to me by a person suspected of witchcraft and she had no evidence except it was some type of vision that she had experienced," Leshoward said.

"I completely understand."

"So you cannot blame yourself. Genevieve has revealed in confidence to me that Penberthy was a traitor during the war. An undiscovered loyalist."

198

"And you think that is justification?"

"No of course not. It is just more information. I want you to believe you cannot hold yourself to blame," Leshoward said.

"It is not Penberthy's blood I have on my hands, although he was the traitor from the war I hesitated to expose before the gala. There is one who met death at my hands near the beginning of these events."

"What? Who?"

"I killed Hortense Melton."

Leshoward was stunned.

Just when he thought he understood everything.

He had stayed away from the question of who killed Hortense, suspecting Genevieve.

"Can you live with me, knowing that?" asked Abigail, after she explained in detail how she had killed Hortense in the printer's shop.

"How many men do you think I killed on the battlefield?"

"That's different."

"Were you not fighting for your life?"

"Yes, I was."

"Were you not fighting for your country?"

"Yes."

"Then there was no difference. Wars are not fought on the battlefield alone. Nor by men only. But by whole peoples in every way they can think of, in every way necessary," Leshoward said.

"I have been much in contemplation since the incident. I'm afraid I fell down on the job and let Genevieve carry most of the burden," said Abigail.

"Tell me," said Leshoward.

"After killing Hortense, I had to get help in moving her body. It could not be left in the print shop. So I went to Fabric. He took the body to the Melton estate and arranged her in the porch swing, thinking she would be found there."

"Ruthanne found her the night she arrived," Leshoward said.

"Yes, I did not get the news about any of this. I was in seclusion, searching for a solution to my life."

"Were you there this entire time? Even before the gala?"

"I rode over to the convent by the river and stayed with the nuns. Except for having to make appearances at some of the Weaving Mistress meetings, I spent as much time there as possible. I had to deal with what I did. That was the right place to do so."

"All the time we could not find you. I've invented many fictional trials to give me an excuse to go off looking for you. So all of this time you were either living as a Weaving Mistress or a Catholic nun?"

Leshoward looked again at this woman he was offering his life to. For a moment she appeared just as she had right before the battle. Young and enigmatic.

Same fair skin, clear gray eyes with a hint of hazel.

"A solution to your life? So a coven or a convent?" he said.

She suddenly grabbed him and held him close.

"Neither. Instead a covenant..."

Chapter 58

To be put forward as nominee for the next Congress.

Hayward suspected that that was why he had been called to this meeting at the tea parlor.

Attending was the new government official sent to replace General Leshoward. He was not a military man but rather some type of bureaucrat with an obscure title that threatened to transform into an official title once statehood was achieved.

In addition, the new mayor, newly elected as the city had finalized its governmental structure, appeared. And Reverend Falldrem was there. Also, Father McKinsy, Mannstein, and surprisingly a woman, Jane Penberthy.

Jane's presence was tolerated with cordiality. A widow in her position would surely soon marry a person of the proper status and then her husband would take her place and the group would be all male again.

She was planning an extensive visit to Philadelphia, as there was no suitable Protestant man of sufficient wealth in the Fort Leverage town area.

Mannstein had sent off to Germany for a Catholic wife.

Mrs. Penberthy no longer smiled at him.

Some small talk began the gathering. Grief was expressed for Reginald. Shock was expressed that Margaret Craig was part of the conspiracy to kill him. Curiosity about Thistle Mannstein and Ruthanne Webber crept in.

Then the group got down to business. The reason they had come together one more time in Fort Leverage. The newcomer spoke first.

"Mr. Manchester, I would like an honest answer. Suppose we tell you that circumstances can be made to conform to a situation where you get the nomination for the congressional seat."

Hayward stood up, then sat back down again.

"Of course we cannot guarantee against unexpected events," said the bureaucrat. "But tell me truly, did you kill with a single one of your swords 27 redcoats?"

Hayward rolled his eyes.

Chapter 59

"I've asked your father for your hand in marriage and he has consented," said Major Plate.

"And now you are telling me?" Lantern smiled as she placed the last of her art supplies in a shipping container.

"Well, yes."

"Father and Abigail have already been married by Reverend Falldrem and they are leaving to go to the plantation. We've already sent a messenger ahead to Harkin that they are coming. I think my father wants to raise horses. The Melton estate is dissolved and there are many horses for sale cheap. It's just a matter of getting them across the state," Lantern said.

"That can be done. Horses have four good legs."

"Right. But since he is being relieved of command and retiring from the Army, we have to decide- you have to decide- what we do," Lantern said.

"I'm considering leaving the army."

"Indeed? I thought you loved the army."

"Also, I will soon be 24. I'm getting a little old. Peace seems to be prevalent. Little chance for advancement or glory and action."

Lantern thought about his large family in Virginia.

"Then have you written to your parents and told them you were coming back?" Lantern asked.

"I've written to my family. In fact, I have actually had time to hear back from them. They are wishing me the best of luck and hope that someday we can visit them before too long. Alternatively, they will come visit us. They are quite healthy and not bad off."

"I don't understand," Lantern said.

"They have two other sons and four daughters, six grandchildren already, more coming and a great-grandchild from my oldest sister whose name I cannot even remember," said Major Plate.

"Of course, you can."

"Okay, I can. But they hardly miss me and I can learn to like horses, Lantern."

"'You don't mean-"

"The general has kindly offered to let us come with him to his lands," said Major Plate.

"To work with horses. What would you do?" Lantern asked.

"Where there are horses, there are horse thieves," said Major Plate.

"So you would be sort of like a horse thief- what, soldier?"

"Well, I would attempt to track down any thieves who stole any horses, but mainly I would be trying to prevent the horses from being taken in the first place."

"Oh, like a guard, or sort of. Like they have at palaces," Lantern said.

"Yes."

"You know, I was considering that I could go on alone. That is if you did want to go see your parents," Lantern said.

"You have only your father and your brother and no way could I ever see you travel all alone."

"You do know, as my older brother, Harkin will be the heir."

"I know as the general's daughter and son-in-law, we might not have the same status as his son and daughter-in-law, but on the other hand the new Mrs. Leshoward is but barely beyond 30, borne no past children to wear her out, and is otherwise quite healthy. So the inheritance may be spread around anyway. Times have changed."

"You know, I hadn't thought of that. And Harkin's wife is already expecting. Father is only 47. What say, if he should live to General Washington's age? And see his grandchildren grown?"

"The general assures me that the house is very large and there's enough room for privacy for several different families."

"Oh heavens! I am going to be living in a large house with a lot of children," Lantern said.

"Some of them ours, I hope."

"God help me."

Chapter 60

"So I am to marry you and it is possible I will bear your child. I think I am entitled to know what your ancestry is. Some darker German perhaps? When you look past being a congressman and think of the senate or the presidency, we will have to account."

The house inside the fort now hers, Genevieve addressed the man soon to move in with her.

Hayward looked down at his bronzed hands, attributed as such to his constant exposure to the sun.

"I've told you about my Indian great-grandfather. The rumors that perhaps Asian blood mingled with Indian blood in those long past times are not anything more than rumors. I know in the past my family had slaves but I don't think they were African. Too long ago. They didn't keep any records. I don't honestly know where my sword making ability comes from. My father was good. My grandfather was good. I am better. Perhaps it's inherited. Perhaps a gift from God. Perhaps a combination of both."

"I see," said Genevieve.

"However-"

"However?" Genevieve asked.

"However, if I am going to dwell inside for long periods of time then we need to think of a way to explain why my skin does not fade to white for lack of exposure to the sun like everybody else's does."

Genevieve took a deep breath and contemplated if the sly look she was getting from her betrothed was indicative that he was teasing her or not.

She looked at his skin, so smooth and consistent in coloration.

"I figure I can settle for being a congressman's wife," Genevieve said.

"Then, I will settle for being a congressman and we will be happy," Hayward said.

"When you are a congressman, you may meet Mr. Jefferson."

"True."

"Do not say anything to him about me."

"Well, you have those papers saying you are his agent. So all you will have to do is bring them out if anybody makes any insinuations about your relationship," Hayward said.

"True. I had not thought of that. I forgot about those papers," Guinevere said not quite truthfully. *I'll have to burn them soon before anybody gets a good look at them,* she thought silently.

"What about children. Will you worry?"

"How important are children?" Genevieve asked.

"Well, not at all to me. I did not ever even plan to marry. But I am told women do not consider themselves complete without them."

"Heavens. I don't even like them. What if we don't have any? Now I don't mean- I mean there are ways to control it- to stop it."

"I know. I am part Indian, remember. There's counting the moon and Abigail Fichton is not the only herbalist in Kentucky," Hayward said.

"So we agree then? You recall I did let it out that you were of French royal descent, albeit not on the right side of the bed. Hope that is okay?" Genevieve asked.

"French royalty? Sounded good to me. Did I contradict you?"

"It might come in handy some bright day if I ever am employed again. And I had to give some reason why you were a target of the assassins. But I do need to know the truth. So do we agree?"

"Agree. And why was I the target?"

"I have no idea. I was going to ask you. Margaret Craig knew you were the real target. I wonder if she is the only one who thought you were behind that mask of the Swedish king."

"You mean you think she was not told the costume assignation had been changed?"

"That's exactly what I believe after thinking it over. We don't know what she or Prudence really knew. All that nonsense about how she could not bear to think she had killed Penberthy- Lantern related those theories to me. Ridiculous! I believe Margaret thought she was killing you. So the question is why."

"I don't have a clue. Unless they saw my skills in creating weaponry as a threat," Hayward said. "I have some interesting ideas concerning guns. Innovations that could change war tactics if they work. I may have been indiscreet in mentioning them in the past."

Genevieve leant towards genealogy rather than creativity as the explanation. She did not press the point.

"They saw your coming into the powerful group as a threat, no doubt. We may never know the reason. Then again it may come back to haunt us. Yes, best we not have any children."

"If we change our minds, well, you might expect a child that will not be blond haired and blue eyed. Some chance of darker than me perhaps."

"Children are real. I can't forge them like papers, unfortunately."

"And I cannot make them to order," Hayward said. "So our children might ruin our chances in high society. I don't think it will be within our lifetime that this country would accept a person in government with an ambiguous ancestry."

"You may be right. But I think there is a mystique in this land that will rise up and make itself known," said Genevieve.

"A mystique?"

"Yes, a mystique. Interwoven within the cloth of our nation. And in the centuries to come and ultimately we will dominate the world."

"That truly does sound like witchcraft," Hayward said.

"Does, sort of, doesn't it?" Genevieve commented.

"It would be interesting to see," Hayward said.

"It would be wonderful to see."

"I'm not sure it would be the completely positive dream that you hold," Hayward said.

"I do. I feel the mystique will penetrate the land and take hold and in times of peril of freedom, it will be there within the fabric of our society, clay within the sands of our land. When there are hard times it will support us, in times of strength shape us to a greater destiny than we can imagine right now here in 1792."

"What is that?"

Hayward's practical question dampened Genevieve's poetic mood.

"Lantern's cloak. She left it here. No curfews where she is going," she said.

Genevieve pulled a sealed envelope from the pocket.

"Looks official. Open it and read it," said Hayward.

"Now that my uncle has gone out west, I suppose I can open this and read it. He said he believed the official notification about the attempted assassination of the King of Sweden was delivered. This looks like it."

Genevieve took the parchment and looked at the official seal. She looked up at Hayward questioningly.

"I'm going to be a congressman. It should not matter if you break the seal," he said.

"You haven't won the election yet but-"

Genevieve unsealed the envelope as Hayward watched with amused interest.

"What does it say?"

"It is news about the assassination attempt on the King of Sweden," said Genevieve.

"Is that a message saying they found a connection?"

"No, exactly the opposite. It says to disregard prior warnings, no connection to any plots against anyone in the United States. And-" Genevieve broke off and bit her lip.

"And what?"

"Yes. They did add a postscript," said Genevieve.

"And? So?"

"They noted the King did not recover. After two weeks, his wound became infected. He died."

Chapter 61

Almost 100 miles away in western Kentucky, Abigail slowly unpacked a few personal belongings in the room she would now be sharing with her new husband.

After a safe arrival the frontier welcomed them with a light late spring frost.

She was in a large bright bedroom with a lovely stone fireplace that was keeping the room warm and glowing.

She made sure her husband was occupied with the arrival of the first of the horses before she continued.

He was earnestly greeting each equine as it came in, with his son by his side. Abigail could even see Lantern and Shears Plate on the lawn beneath the window.

Still, she locked her door before approaching a shabby valise.

She opened up the old suitcase. She pulled out an old faded silhouette of a young soldier and put it away in a drawer. A small miniature of President Washington, she displayed on the fireplace mantle.

Then she went back to her luggage and pulled out a long black robe.

She gave a little sad sigh as she carefully folded it and doused it with a little oil before tossing it into the fireplace. She did likewise with a matching headpiece.

A shower of sparks flew at her as the material went up in smoke.

Then she opened up an old book and placed it on a small table by the bed.

She knelt, put her hand on the book, and lifted her other hand upwards, audibly reciting her words from memory.

"Oh Lord God
Upon whom I call
Grant peace to our land
Grant healing to us all."

Published by Ruskras Corner

Historical Fiction Mysteries- by Deborah DR Kralich

1790s era

The Mystique Woven in Our Land

1900s era

Murder as the Organist Plays

1930s era

Interlude of Carelessness

Historical Fiction- 1960s era

The Mystery of the Missing Persons

Lt. Plate Series- 1980s era

An Innovative Murder for the Season

The Ruler of the Toys

A Kaleidoscope of Masquerades

The Unknown Puppeteer

Short Stories anthology

Poised Like a Knife

Poetry

I Lift Up My Heart

Humorous Science Fiction/Fantasy

3748 AD- The Return of the Cat by Carl S. Kralich

Auction of Worlds- by Carl S. Kralich

A Cat Whisperer- by Deborah Denise

www.ingramcontent.com/pod-product-compliance
Lightning Source LLC
Chambersburg PA
CBHW061155170626
46809CB00003B/1106